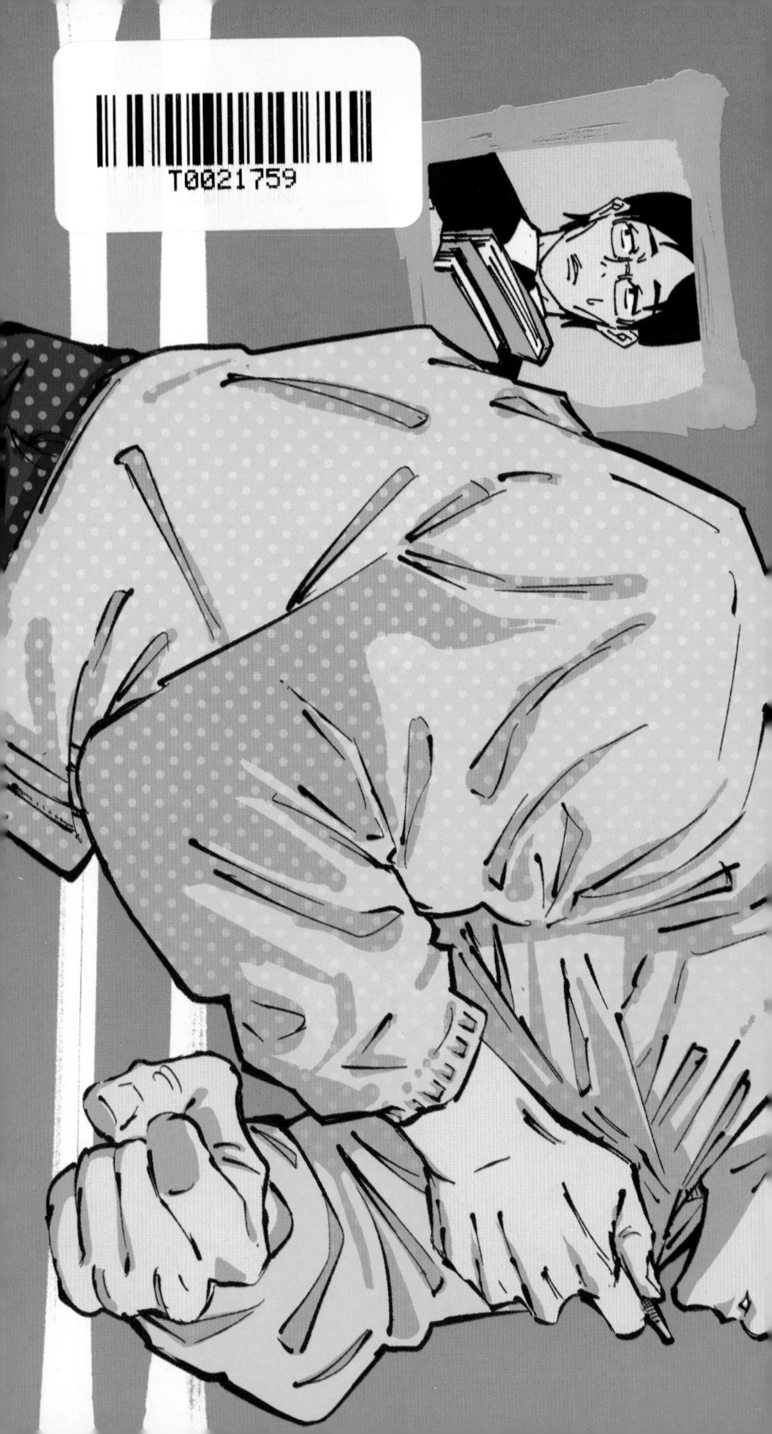

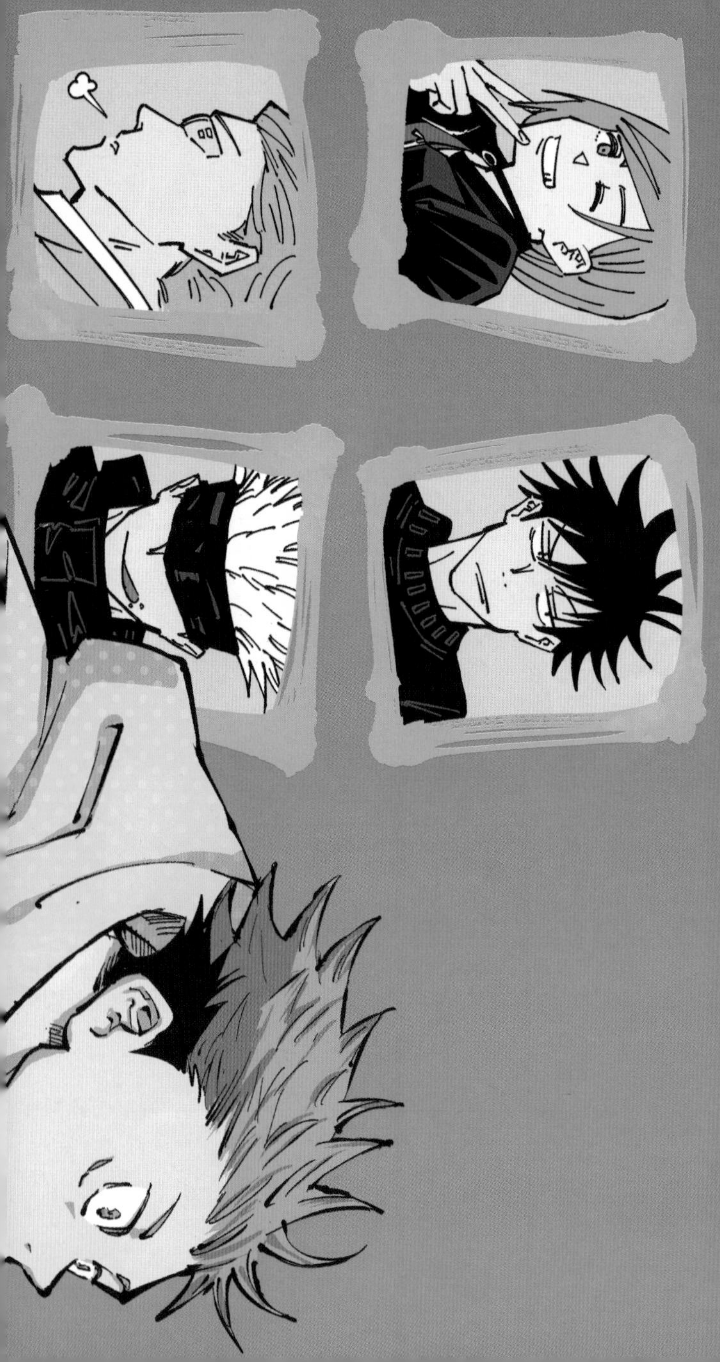

JUJUTSU KAISEN

Summer of Ashes, Autumn of Dust

CREATED BY
GEGE AKUTAMI

NOVEL BY
BALLAD KITAGUNI

Special Grade Cursed Spirit

Mahito

Jujutsu High First-Year

Megumi Fushiguro

Grade 1 Sorcerer

Kento Nanami

Jujutsu High Assistant Manager

Kiyotaka Ijichi

Jujutsu High First-Year

Yuji Itadori

Special Grade Jujutsu Sorcerer

Satoru Gojo

—CURSE—

Hardship, regret, shame... The misery that comes from these negative human emotions can lead to death.

Yuji Itadori is an athletically gifted student who doesn't care much about school. However, one fateful day, in order to protect his school from a curse, he swallows the severed finger of the legendary demon Ryomen Sukuna! Now Itadori is host to the soul of the most infamous demon in human history. Itadori expects to be executed, but thanks to Satoru Gojo, he instead ends up at Tokyo Prefectural Jujutsu High School, an institution that specializes in fighting curses. Alongside his classmates Fushiguro and Kugisaki, he begins studying jujutsu...

JUJUTSU KAISEN
Summer of Ashes, Autumn of Dust

GEGE AKUTAMI

Born in 1992 in Iwate Prefecture. In 2014, Akutami began his professional manga career with *Kamishiro Sosa* (God Age Investigation), but this cat's claws didn't make much of a mark.

As a child, Akutami habitually fibbed, filched food, broke things, and blamed the dog. Thus, when Akutami came home after actually getting hit by a car, no one believed him.

At the time of this writing, in 2019, *Jujutsu Kaisen* was being serialized in *Weekly Shonen Jump*. There seems to be a general consensus that it's been drawn in a style people have seen somewhere before.

BALLAD KITAGUNI

Born in 19×× in Hokkaido. In 2015, Kitaguni began pushing certain idiosyncrasies on the world with *Apricot Red*.

One time in the summer, Kitaguni forgot that he had thrust a chocolate bar into a pocket that also contained a smartphone. When Kitaguni pulled out the phone later, it was dripping and gooey, causing an appalled friend to ask, "What did you just give birth to?!"

At the time of this writing, in 2019, Kitaguni was so absorbed in the *Jujutsu Kaisen* graphic novels he was sent as reference material for this book that he ended up buying all the digital editions too.

JUJUTSU KAISEN
Summer of Ashes, Autumn of Dust

JUJUTSU KAISEN YUKU NATSU TO KAERU AKI
© 2019 by Gege Akutami, Ballad Kitaguni
All rights reserved.
First published in Japan in 2019 by SHUEISHA Inc., Tokyo.
English translation rights arranged by SHUEISHA Inc.

COVER AND INTERIOR DESIGN Shawn Carrico
TRANSLATION John Werry
EDITOR Megan Bates

Published by VIZ Media, LLC
P.O. Box 77010
San Francisco, CA 94107

Library of Congress Cataloging-in-Publication Data

Names: Kitaguni, Ballad, writer. | Akutami, Gege, 1992- creator. | Werry,
John (Translator), translator.
Title: Jujutsu Kaisen : summer of ashes, autumn of dust / created by Gege
Akutami ; written by Baraddo Kitaguni ; translation, John Werry.
Other titles: Jujutsu Kaisen. English
Description: San Francisco, CA : Viz Media, 2022. | Summary: "Cursed
spirits have struck the opening blow at Satozakura High School in an
unfolding conflict against the Jujutsu Sorcerers, but while this epic
and unyielding battle intensifies, the heroes of Jujutsu Kaisen have
other mysteries to solve."-- Provided by publisher.
Identifiers: LCCN 2022018507 (print) | LCCN 2022018508 (ebook) | ISBN
9781974732555 (paperback) | ISBN 9781974735921 (ebook)
Subjects: CYAC: Fantasy. | Supernatural--Fiction. | Demonology--Fiction. |
Magic--Fiction. | Wizards--Fiction. | LCGFT: Paranormal fiction. |
Action and adventure fiction. | Light novels.
Classification: LCC PZ7.1.K627 Ju 2022 (print) | LCC PZ7.1.K627 (ebook) |
DDC [Fic]--dc23
LC record available at https://lccn.loc.gov/2022018507
LC ebook record available at https://lccn.loc.gov/2022018508

Printed in the U.S.A.
First Printing, December 2022

viz.com

CHAPTER 1 Kyujitsu Kaisen

Few things are certain in this day and age. At most, only three: Mito Komon always wins, *Sazae* airs on Sundays, and Nobara Kugisaki takes forever to shop.

So when Kugisaki said she wanted to see Ameya-Yokocho, Fushiguro was ready for a long haul, similar to one of those Sunday mornings when Gojo would say, "Megumi, shall we go to Parque España?"

Because of Itadori's love of TV, Fushiguro expected him to be interested in a trendy destination, but he wasn't. Instead, he said, "No, there's someplace else I want to go."

"Oh, all right. Then let's meet up later."

Fushiguro, who had become accustomed to the boisterous mood Itadori and Kugisaki generated when they were together, was as surprised by the trio splitting up as if he had found out that *hijiki* was low in iron, and pleased. He wanted to go straight home to finish reading the paperback he'd bought the other day, and he wanted to organize his desk drawer and closet.

However, Fushiguro was the serious, responsible type. He worried whether Itadori, a vessel for the demon Sukuna, would be okay on his own. The district of Ueno around Okachimachi Station was both historical and hopping with activity. An abundance of peculiar tales of the supernatural were associated with the lively postwar market town, so dormant curses might well be lurking there. Even worse, if Fushiguro took his eyes off him for even a second, Itadori might buy a pair of horribly tacky sunglasses or declare Tachikawa to be the essence of Shinjuku. He might even wander into Chiyoda Ward and start snapping pics at Masakado's tomb to post on social media.

Thus, loathe though he was to do it, Fushiguro decided to stay with Itadori.

"Fushiguro, if you aren't interested in Akiba, why're you coming along?" Itadori asked.

"Mind your own business."

"Fine," Itadori responded. "Anyway, I always did wanna check out Akiba."

"Is there something you want to buy?" Fushiguro asked. "I doubt there's anything more than manga, video games, and electronics."

"Huh? I'm going sightseeing," Itadori said. "Shibuya and Shinjuku are all right, but whenever I see Akiba on TV, it has a real otherworldly vibe, sort of like a theme park."

"So that's your reason, huh?"

Those who are used to living in the city might not notice it, but Akihabara is an odd place. The atmosphere around the station is unique. It's drenched in anime culture, and the sheer volume of visual stimulus from the ubiquitous advertisements is astounding. The abundance of flashing signs featuring smiling video game characters do indeed give the whole district the impression of a theme park. Other sights might include an occasional cosplayer amidst the densely packed crowd, maids busily handing out flyers to attract customers to the maid cafés, or an unusual foreign automobile cruising down the road transporting a large prototype of a giant robot.

Itadori was unable to suppress his curiosity in such a place. It was impossible.

"This is crazy, Fushiguro! There are game centers everywhere! They're like convenience stores!"

"Because this is Akiba."

"This is crazy, Fushiguro! Those maids are actually trying to get our attention!"

"Because this is Akiba."

"This is crazy, Fushiguro! Is that a pervy video game? That sign is for a pervy game, right? Whoa, is that allowed?! Like, right out in the open! Uh-oh... I'm underage! Will I get in trouble?!"

"Shut up already!"

Akiba is a noisy place, but to Fushiguro, Itadori was three times noisier.

They had a few hours before they were to meet back up with Kugisaki. Fushiguro's head hurt just thinking about spending all that time in Akiba alone with Itadori, who had transformed into a wide-eyed child. Itadori, meanwhile, was in high spirits, oblivious to Fushiguro's mood.

"I'm so glad you came, Fushiguro!" Itadori said. "It's so crowded I might get lost!"

"But it's not as crowded as Shinjuku, right?"

"Don't judge it by the usual Tokyo standards," Itadori responded. "Tokyo's the only place where vending machines that accept electronic money are lined up all over the place and Pepper's standing around in front of all the stores!"

"Seeing a Pepper robot isn't that common," Fushiguro said.

"In Sendai, the only thing to see is the artificial hot spring Topos."

"Don't casually drop your local joints into the conversation like I'm supposed to know what you're talking about. What is that Topos place like, anyway?"

"It's a superdeluxe public bath!"

"If Pepper standing at a public bath is a sign of civilization, we're in trouble."

"Anyway," Itadori said. "I'm just saying that instead of being alone, it's reassuring to be with someone who knows the terrain. After all, I'm still not great at taking the subway."

"Not even you could get lost on the Yamanote Line!" Fushiguro said.

"There it is! That city-boy attitude! It comes to you so naturally!"

"Actually, you don't get lost that much anymore. You go places all the time."

"Hey, Fushiguro!" Itadori exclaimed. "Let's eat a kebab. Kebaaab!"

"Try to make sense, would you?!"

Fushiguro had already noticed that Itadori and Gojo had a similar vibe, and the more he talked to him, the stronger that impression got. With Itadori, conversation was less like playing catch than dodgeball. In Gojo's case, it was like swinging away on a golf course or at a batting center.

It occurred to Fushiguro that he hadn't seen Gojo around the dorm or Tokyo Prefectural Jujutsu High School that day. Gojo could go wherever he wanted on a day off, but Fushiguro found himself wondering once again about the many mysteries surrounding the teacher. As he did so, he let Itadori's chattering drift into the background. It resonated at about the same frequency as the clamorous streets and so was easy to tune out. The next thing he knew, Itadori was gone.

"Huh?"

Fushiguro looked around in confusion and spotted Itadori's reddish hair just as it disappeared into a game center.

"What are you doing?"

"Playing a video game. Or do you mean what *game* am I playing?" Itadori asked.

"No, you special grade dunce!"

Fushiguro had finally located Itadori after climbing to the fourth floor of a game center located in a tall, narrow structure. Itadori was deep in the fighting-game area, at a slight remove from a gathering of hard-core gamers, in a corner lined with retro cabinet arcade games with prices starting at fifty yen for one credit.

Even worse, he was sitting in front of a game that looked particularly dull, even compared to its neighbors.

Itadori pursed his lips and launched into an explanation. "It doesn't make sense to spend hours wandering around outside. But there are tons of game centers, which is perfect!"

"At least say something before you wander off!"

"I did."

"Ah…" Fushiguro felt a twinge of guilt for tuning out Itadori earlier, so he changed the subject. "Anyway, what game *is* that?"

"Isn't it obvious? It's *Combat Corporate Warriors Business Fighter*."

"*Combat Corporate Warriors Business Fighter*? That's anything but obvious."

"It's my first time, so I don't know much about it either," said Itadori.

The game Itadori had chosen seemed unbelievably boring. Although it was a fighting game, most of the characters looked to be middle-aged company men. They all wore business suits, which made it hard to tell them apart. It only cost fifty yen, but still, that Itadori had chosen this game out of all the games here was mind-boggling.

No wonder he ate Suzuna's finger, Fushiguro thought.

Itadori kept playing. "Wanna play? It's a two-player setup."

"I refuse to pay for that game." Fushiguro frowned as if experiencing something truly distasteful.

But one-on-one fighting games are only as fun as your opponent. And playing such a mind-numbing game alone was pointless. Despite Fushiguro's reluctance, Itadori really wanted to play him.

"Huh? Are you too chicken? Or do you suck at video games, Fushiguro? Afraid you can't beat me?" Itadori said.

"I'm *not* afraid. I just don't feel like it."

"If you chicken out, that's a loss by default! A defeat! Are you really fine with that?!"

"Play by yourself," said Fushiguro.

"Come on, I'm begging you! I'll even pay for you! Okay?"

"Are you serious? Ugh…"

Itadori started fishing out some change, but Fushiguro put in his own money and sat at the opposing screen. Perhaps he had crumbled in the face of Itadori's persistence, or maybe he just didn't want to watch him grovel.

After all, fighting games *are* more fun with two players than one.

Itadori, who was immensely grateful to Fushiguro for joining, cheerfully selected his character. "All right, I'm President Yamada."

"And…I'm Subsection Manager Osaki," Fushiguro said.

"Seriously? That's the default starting character! Well, he's probably easy to use, so he's perfect for a beginner like *you*, Fushiguro."

"Didn't you say this is *your* first time too?"

"Well, before you got here, I made it to the third screen in arcade mode," Itadori boasted.

"Sounds weak to me."

The two began playing.

"Take that!" Itadori said. "In just fifteen minutes I've developed a technique for certain victory!"

"What a short training period."

Itadori began by attacking with a barrage of Business Card Shuriken, which only required a simple command. Meanwhile, Fushiguro had Subsection Manager Osaki jump to avoid President Yamada's shuriken bursts as he closed the distance. Then he executed a sudden dive into a strong kick, which he followed by throwing his opponent against the wall and delivering a flurry of blows.

"Huh? Hold on, Fushiguro! You've got me pinned! No fair!"

"Uh…"

Light punch, light punch, medium kick, medium kick… Fushiguro built up his Overtime Gauge through a vicious onslaught and then used it to finish off his opponent with the killer technique Fists of Overtime Fury.

It was a brilliant victory.

"No way! What the...?! Fushiguro! How'd you know that special move?! Are you actually *good* at this game?!"

"There's a list of controls over the screen."

"You cheated!" Itadori said.

"Maybe you're just no good at video games."

"Well, if I'd known the commands, I wouldn't have lost! Let's play again! One more round!"

"Give me a break," Fushiguro said. "Are you really putting in more coins?"

After a full hour of combat, Itadori had more losses than wins.

The two of them were feeling drained as they went down to the floor with the crane games and bought a couple of sodas from the vending machines. After the heat of battle had cooled, they felt something like a comedown, and the decrease in their energy levels was evident on their faces.

"Aw... Why did I waste a thousand yen on that dumb game?" Itadori hung his head.

Fushiguro looked at him like he was an utter fool. "If you're satisfied now, let's get out of here. Game centers are good for passing time, but they'll also eat up your cash."

"That's for sure. Oh, hey!"

"What? If you've found another ridiculous game you want to play, I will not be not joining you this time," Fushiguro said.

"No, that's not it. Look, Fushiguro! Over there!"

Fushiguro narrowed his eyes and reluctantly turned in the direction Itadori was pointing. His eyes widened in surprise. "Gojo Sensei?"

"Yeah, that's him," Itadori said.

Without a doubt, the person they were looking at was none other than Satoru Gojo. After all, who but Gojo would stroll around in the dim light of a game center wearing black clothes with a black blindfold over his eyes?

"Huh? Um, Fushiguro? What is Gojo Sensei doing?"

"He's playing a crane game," Fushiguro said. "To win snacks."

"But why? He came to a game center alone to play crane games because he got the *munchies*?!"

"Hey, don't ask me," replied Fushiguro. "How should *I* know?"

"Oh," said Itadori. "He gave up!"

"That was fast."

Pouting in dissatisfaction, Gojo swaggered toward the game center's exit.

His behavior was hard to understand, but Gojo had always been hard to understand. Fushiguro decided not to think about it too much.

Itadori had other ideas. "Let's follow him," he said.

"And why would we do that?"

Itadori was making as if to dart out of the game center in pursuit of Gojo. In a rush, Fushiguro gulped down his soda, threw away the can, and followed.

"Think about it," Itadori said. "Gojo Sensei is probably off today, right? And I don't know what he does on his days off or in his free time!"

"So?"

"So we follow him!"

"You say that like it makes sense," said Fushiguro.

"Well, I'm curious! I know next to nothing about Gojo Sensei. Of course, if you don't want to, you can wait here *alone*."

"Ah..."

Fushiguro and Itadori ended up tailing Gojo.

There was no doubt Gojo was a reliable teacher and a respectable sorcerer. To the students, however, he was also a man of many mysteries due to his nonchalance, busy demeanor, unpredictability, career, way of thinking, and scale of activity. He didn't seem like the kind to cheerily stroll about town on his days off.

In other words, Fushiguro gave in to *his* curiosity too.

Also, fighting Itadori in that dumb game may have left him mentally exhausted. In any case, they lost sight of Gojo and started looking for him again.

They found him with little difficulty.

"Fushiguro, there's Gojo."

"Yes, I see."

When they spotted Gojo this time, he was eating a crepe as he walked. Judging by the paper wrapping, the crepe was from a well-known shop facing a main street. It was a sizable creation, with whipped cream, tiramisu, macarons, and even chocolate drizzle. Gojo was a six-foot-two adult munching on what looked like a child's dream confection.

"I'm impressed, Fushiguro," Itadori said. "I wouldn't even know how to order that!"

"Who would *want* to?"

"Maybe it's some kind of jujutsu training?"

"How nice it would be if we could power up that way!"

The two kept their distance as they followed the guy gobbling a crepe. Even on the strange streets of Akihabara, they must have stood out. Before long, Gojo finished his crepe and stopped in front of a sorely rundown shop.

Itadori read the sign above the shop door. "Vacuum tube specialty shop..."

Gojo pondered for a moment, then stepped into the cluttered establishment.

"He has some unusual interests," Fushiguro said, looking perplexed.

Itadori cocked his head. "I've heard of vacuum tubes, but what *are* they?"

"A piece of electronics from old radios and audio equipment."

"Is Gojo Sensei an audiophile?"

"No," Fushiguro said. "He seems more like the kind of guy who listens to music on YouTube."

"Yeah, I bet you're right!"

As Itadori and Fushiguro were talking, Gojo came out of the shop holding a paper bag. Apparently, he had purchased something.

"Uh-oh. We're losing him."

With Fushiguro in tow, Itadori turned down an alley, following Gojo. They were slow enough to respond that they couldn't see Gojo at that point, but within seconds they spied a tall figure in black amidst the crowd.

"There he is, Fushiguro. Gojo Sensei is hard to miss. He's huge!"

"Yes, over six feet."

"He'd rule on the basketball court."

"Although I can't imagine him playing basketball," Fushiguro said.

"Me neither!"

Having reached agreement on this point, the two of them continued their pursuit. Following someone at a distance through the convoluted streets of Akihabara was arduous work. Gojo was tall, so his stride was long and he walked fast. If Itadori and Fushiguro had stepped out of the crowd on the sidewalk, they would immediately have lost track of him.

Gojo's next stop was a used music shop, where he perused vinyl records in paper jackets.

"Despite what you said, Fushiguro, Gojo Sensei may actually be a music geek," Itadori said.

"No, I doubt that."

"But he's looking at records. Bach, no less!"

"Does that look like a guy who'd be interested in classical music?" asked Fushiguro.

"No, more like alternative rock."

"Exactly," Fushiguro said. "So this is definitely weird."

After crate diving for a while, Gojo bought an LP of soundtrack music from an old foreign film and left the shop.

Itadori and Fushiguro became increasingly suspicious as they continued tailing him.

Momentarily, they started to believe that they may have misjudged Gojo and that he really *did* have a taste for classical music, but they quickly came to their senses and dismissed the thought.

Gojo moseyed along, then stopped in front of a shop with a yellow sign.

"Fushiguro, what kind of store is that?" Itadori asked.

"It sells capsule toys," Fushiguro said. "It's a *gachapon* shop."

"What? Stores like that exist?"

"In Akiba, they do."

"Oh, okay. Look, he's getting one!"

"I really don't need to see one of my teachers buying a 500-yen capsule toy," Fushiguro said. "But what machine did he choose?"

"It has keychains that look like mushrooms. Realistic ones."

"If you're going to spend 500 yen, wouldn't it be better to get *real* mushrooms at the supermarket?"

"You don't understand, Fushiguro. Capsule toys are great because you never know what you'll get!"

"I hope I never do understand that."

"He opened it! What'd he get?!" Itadori asked.

"It looks like he got a poisonous mushroom, and he doesn't seem pleased."

"Bwa ha ha ha ha ha ha! He can't eat *that* mushroom!!"

"You can't eat any of the mushrooms. They're toys!"

Gojo grumpily tucked the keychain into a pocket and resumed his peregrination.

He went into a computer shop and fiddled with a mouse. Then he went into an electronics shop and tried a massage device on his shoulders. They lost track of him for a bit before finding him again reading manga in a bookstore. Then he swayed down a side street to peruse used video games at a sidewalk sale. Apparently, he was going wherever his whims led.

"He doesn't appear to have any specific purpose," Fushiguro noted.

"Nope, doesn't seem like it," Itadori responded, now wearing toy goggles that claimed to measure combat strength.

"Where did you buy those?"

"Some secondhand shop. When I saw Gojo reading manga, I thought he might like these."

"Do you ever keep your wallet closed?"

"Men splurge when something catches their eye," Itadori said.

"And that stupid game earlier caught your eye?"

"Hey! Gojo went into a building! Or rather, his *ki* did."

"You didn't need to rephrase that."

"Uh-oh! We're losing him. C'mon, Fushiguro!"

Itadori took a step toward the building's entrance, but Fushiguro stopped him by yanking on the hood of his hoodie. (This is dangerous, so you should never do it to your friends.)

"No, not so fast."

"Are you trying to kill me?" Itadori demanded. "What's the problem? Did we follow him all the way here only to give up?"

"Didn't you see the sign on the building?"

"Huh?" Itadori looked up and read the sign. "Oh!"

ANGEL MAID CAFÉ MISCHIEVOUS ☆ CUPID!

The second floor of the building was home to a café that catered to a clientele with very specific tastes. It wasn't a *lewd* establishment, exactly. It was just a wholesome café...where the servers dressed like maids. Going inside a place like that required a degree of fortitude, especially if you were a boy of a certain age. Even Itadori could feel his cheeks turning red.

"This is unexpected. Even for Gojo," he said.

"Maybe he came for *these*." Fushiguro pointed to several flyers posted on the wall advertising "French-style pancakes to make even a pâtissier's mouth water!"

That made sense to Itadori. "That must be it! He eats gobs of sweets!"

"And he does indulge his sweet tooth more when he's going through an especially busy period."

"Well, we solved the mystery, so I guess we can stop following him. I'm too embarrassed to go in there."

"That's a smart decision," responded Itadori. "For you, anyway."

"Welcome, Masters!"

The greeting, bright and eager, came from behind them, and both boys let out sounds of surprise.

Neither Itadori's powerful physical instincts nor Fushiguro's polished curse-detection skills had picked up the approach of a veteran server. She was on the prowl for customers and had snuck up on the two boys. They may have looked hesitant to enter, but she knew a ripe source of income when she saw one.

Fushiguro wondered what he had done in a previous life to deserve this.

Before he could gather his wits, the maid had ushered him and Itadori into the café. Inside, a staff member forced him to put on angel wings and a halo made from plastic and wire. "This is so you get a taste of Heaven!"

Now he both looked and *felt* dead.

"For new masters, we recommend the Sacred Set meal," said the maid. "The Heart-Heart A meal!"

"Huh? Oh, right. Well, it's my first time here, so I suppose it's best to take the staff recommendation. Two Sacred Sets, extra heart," said Itadori.

"Your wish is our karma! ☆"

"Huh? That sounded cool!" Itadori was already warming to the idea of a conversation with the maid. He liked parties and had a sunny disposition, so adapting to new situations came easy for him. For a serious, responsible person, like Fushiguro, it was another matter entirely. Taking in the scene, decked out in a halo and wings, he could feel his soul dying a little.

"Now, back to the crucial matter at hand, Fushiguro," Itadori said.

"Which is?"

"It seems that Sensei really did come here for the pancakes."

Gojo had chosen a window seat with a view of the wall of a neighboring building, and now he was enjoying pancakes and a beverage in a leisurely and somewhat smug manner. He sipped his cappuccino with an attitude straight from a hard-boiled mystery novel, and he wore his angel cosplay like it was some kind of formal attire. The level of relaxation he exhibited was completely at odds with the newbie vibe of Itadori and Fushiguro.

"Okay, we found out what Gojo Sensei's up to," Fushiguro said. "So if you're satisfied, let's get out of here."

"Huh? But we just ordered!"

"We can pay what we owe on our way out."

"But it would be wrong to waste the food," Itadori said.

"Right... I suppose you have a point."

Fushiguro wanted to leave even if it meant paying for nothing, but he was a conscientious person, and he couldn't argue with Itadori's reasoning.

His eyes grew distant, like he was gazing into a ditch in the middle of the night. He considered tuning everything out. For living things, going numb is like a safety switch. If he didn't do something now to protect his mental equilibrium, he might give birth to some kind of curse.

Itadori, meanwhile, seemed jittery but nonetheless appeared to be enjoying the attractions.

However, their true baptism to maid cafés was yet to come.

Their server appeared beside their table. "Thank you for waiting! Here are your Sacred Sets! Heart-Heart A!"

The Sacred Set turned out to be *omurice*, which they could never have guessed from the description on the menu.

On the plate was an illustration of a panda made with ketchup. Perhaps it was a coincidence, but it closely resembled Panda Senpai, which caused an emotional pang within Fushiguro. Below the panda was a caption: Sacred and tired as hell. A reference to the slow-moving panda. Fushiguro agreed that this all was indeed tiring.

Itadori, however, was getting into the mood.

"Masters, I need you to glop on more heart!" said their server.

"How do we do that?" asked Itadori.

"Describe a heartfelt, beloved, or especially dramatic scene from an anime you like without saying the title, and if the heart comes across, you pass!"

"Huh? Whoa... That's hard!" said Itadori. "Okay, um...the main character is a boy who admires heroes."

"I watch that, I watch that! I'm a huge fan!" exclaimed the server.

"And there's a character with a father complex. When he remembers how he wanted to become a hero, he uses his *left* hand, which he wouldn't before. I liked that."

"Ahh, that episode's a classic! But your choice of scene is too cliché. Try again!"

"All right then, a different anime." Itadori thought for a moment. "The main character loses his parents and grows up in a ninja village, and there's a scene where everyone accepts him as worthy and tosses him into the air."

"Yes, that's so *heartful*!"

"You know how his instructor, the only one who was on his side, gets tears in his eyes? That's the best," Itadori said.

"Yes! You're almost there!"

"And he says something like, 'Now, there is a hero before my eyes.'" continued Itadori.

"I totally know what you mean! Totally tons of heart! That super touched me, so I'll give you a free side!" the server said.

"Oh, that's how this works?"

"Fried potatoes usually cost 400 yen, but you can have some Heart Fries for free!"

"Wah ha! Gimme a break! This meal has too many carbohydrates!" Itadori said.

"Now say *h-e-a-r-t-f-u-l* with me!" cheered the server.

"*H-e-a-r-t-f-u-l*!"

The maid dumped fries on his plate.

They were clearly cooked from frozen, not worth anything close to 400 yen. The maid café's usual clientele might not have minded the price, but it bugged Fushiguro. A *lot* of things were bugging Fushiguro.

And now the maid had set her sights on him.

"Hey you. Join the fun!" she said.

"C'mon, Fushiguro," Itadori said. "You'll get a free side too."

"Say *h-e-a-r-t-f-u-l*!" the server instructed.

Itadori did as he was told, but Fushiguro was unresponsive. Yet the fun continued.

"There, I added your extra side. Let's snap a group pic with your meal! Scooch in, scooch in!" the server said.

"Huh? You do photos too?" Itadori asked.

"It's part of the Sacred Set you ordered!"

"Uh… I don't really get it, but okay!"

"Feels like heaven, doesn't it?" she said.

"Dunno. Does it?" Itadori asked. "Yeah, maybe it does!"

"Mind if I plop down beside you?"

Itadori tried to make room, but there was nowhere to go. "Huh? Aren't you a little too close? This is a bit embarrassing."

"This kind of embarrassment is part of growing up!" the server chided.

"It is?"

"Yup! Say *cheese*! ☆"

"Um, cheese!"

"Thanks so much!"

Itadori was beside himself. "Oh man… I'm blushing! Gah!

My face feels hot! I feel like I just lost something important! Is this okay? I'm underage!"

"*Kyah!* Your innocence is adorable! Your friend should join us for another pic!"

"This requires a different sense of personal space than a school dance," Itadori said. "So be careful, Fushiguro. It's really embarrassing! You'll blush like crazy!"

"Prepare for the pic!" the server said.

"No, I..." Fushiguro sounded like a dying duck as he put up a feeble resistance. "That isn't...necessary, so..."

Fushiguro couldn't take it anymore.

"Whoa... I ate more than I expected. It wasn't that tasty though," observed Idatori.

"The fries made my mouth dry," Fushiguro replied sullenly.

Thirty minutes had passed since they'd made it out of Heaven, where, on top of their overpriced food, they'd also had to pay a service charge of 500 yen.

"Fushiguro, I got the photo. Want it?"

"The next time you joke around about that, I'm going to jam red bell peppers up your nose," Fushiguro said.

"You really hated those! Okay, I got it. Now I know the worst way to irritate you."

"There's a shrine around Kanda. We can burn the photo there."

"Why go all the way to a shrine?!" Itadori said.

"Because you have to offer cursed photos to a bonfire."

"Sorry! The maid café was excruciating for you! I get it!"

Fushiguro always seemed crabby, but today he was full-on angry. That made it difficult for Itadori to get into his usual groove. Uncomfortable, he scratched his cheek as he considered how to change the subject.

"H-hey, uh...we lost sight of Gojo Sensei," he said.

"Who cares?"

"N-no, seriously." said Itadori. "Where did he go?"

"What's this about me?"

"*Uwaaah!!*" Fushiguro and Itadori yelped in surprise.

At some point, Gojo had come up behind them, and he wasn't alone: Kugisaki stood beside Gojo with a disgruntled, even threatening look in her eyes.

"G-Gojo Sensei! When did you creep up behind us?! And...huh? Kugisaki's here too? Why?" asked Itadori.

"Do you really have to ask, birdbrain?!" Kugisaki snapped.

"Aw, man! Even Kugisaki is in a bad mood!" Itadori felt like he had picked up another grumpy classmate.

"Of course I am! This is your fault for lurking around Gojo!"

Itadori sensed that Kugisaki's dissatisfaction might manifest in a more physical way than Fushiguro's, so he thought it best to change the subject. "Um...do you have today off, Gojo Sensei?"

"Don't ignore me! *Hmf!*" Kugisaki said.

"No, I'm working as usual," Gojo said.

"Huh? But you were strolling around snacking on a crepe!"

"I'm so busy that if I don't make strolling around town a part of my work, I never get to experience anything new! However it may have looked, I was actually working on something!"

"Like what?" Itadori asked.

"Looking for a dungeon," Gojo said.

"A dungeon?"

"I was scoping out a cursed spot where some first-years could gain some solid experience."

"Um...what?"

Itadori recalled a day not long after he'd enrolled at Jujutsu High when he'd gone out on what he'd thought was a tour of Tokyo, but what turned out to be a mandatory exercise in the form of eradicating cursed spirits from an abandoned building.

Gojo continued. "The building next to that maid café is mostly empty, but it's been the subject of rumors on horror websites and is known for being a haunted spot. An esteemed record shop was located there for many years, which unfortunately lent some credibility to the stories about curses."

"Oh, so that's why you were looking out that window at some building."

"I planned on doing this at a later date, but as luck would have it, I currently have three first-years at my disposal," Gojo said. "So this will be a good challenge for today!"

"Huh? What?!"

"Don't worry. I've already stationed the vacuum tube amps in the building. According to the rumors, playing records agitates the cursed spirits, so I've got that going. So you'll be able to confront cursed spirits that have some *kick*."

"Huh?!"

Itadori glanced at Kugisaki. Now he knew why she looked so displeased. Fushiguro, on the other hand, was the exact opposite: he was stoked.

"Why do you look so eager?!" Itadori asked.

"This sounds a lot more enjoyable than game centers and maid cafés," Fushiguro said.

"Huh? You went to a maid café?" Kugisaki gaped. "Itadori is one thing, but you too, Fushiguro? You play innocent, but you're just a lecherous creep!"

"It was unavoidable," Fushiguro said.

"What do you mean I'm 'one thing'?!" Itadori said.

"Anyway, let's roll out," said Fushiguro.

"Why're you in full battle mode, Fushiguro?!" Kugisaki asked.

"Megumi didn't get a good opportunity to show off his skills in that abandoned building a while ago, so he's been frustrated," explained Itadori.

"I'm *not* frustrated."

"The look on your face says you are."

"You're totally the type to nurse a grudge," Kugisaki piled on.

Ignoring the trio's bickering, Gojo remarked, "Well, take care, everyone. I'm gonna go eat deep-fried *manju*."

"You have room for more, Sensei?!" Itadori and Fushiguro were shocked.

However, Fushiguro felt cheered now that a maddening day off was turning into sorcerer work. "Let's hop to it, guys!"

"No, let's not! Argh! Goodbye to my day off!" cried Itadori.

"And to Ame-Yoko!" added Kugisaki.

Itadori found his interesting day off cut short, and Kugisaki was going to miss out on sampling from the famous Hyakkaen fruit shop at Ame-Yoko. With his usual faint smile, Gojo watched as the three chattered away en route to eradicating cursed spirits.

"Hm?"

Something fell out of Itadori's pocket and fluttered to the ground. Gojo knelt and picked it up. He tilted his head, trying to figure out just what he was looking at. The moment he did, he burst out laughing.

"Heh heh heh heh... For all their moaning and groaning, those kids appear to be enjoying their youth after all!"

He was 80 percent amused by how funny they looked and 20 percent amused about how heartwarming it was.

Gojo stood there for a moment, smiling and holding the photograph of Itadori and Fushiguro in halos and angel wings in the company of a maid.

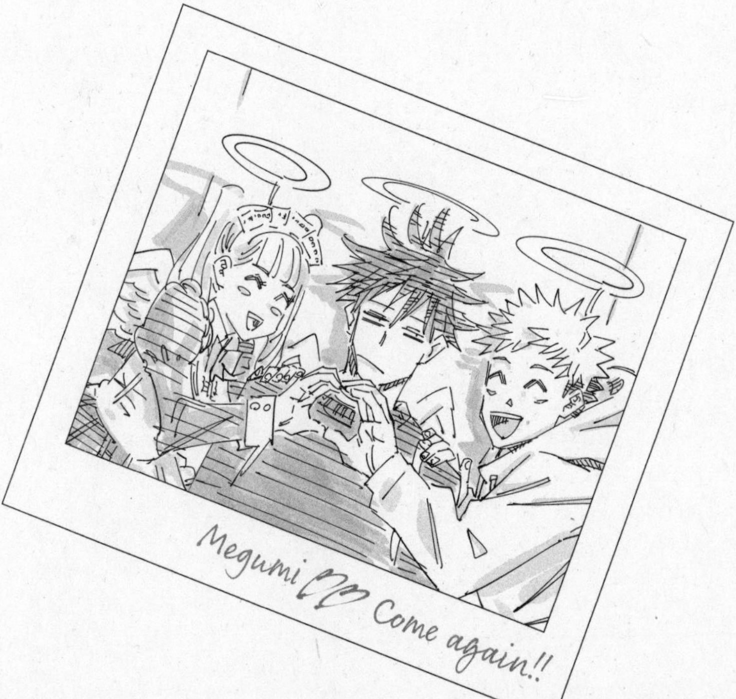
Megumi ♡♡ Come again!!

CHAPTER 2 Resurrection Doll

CHAPTER 2 Resurrection Doll

Nanami didn't mind business trips.

His employer could cover the expenses, and they gave him a reason to go places he might not otherwise go. That this one was to Hokkaido was all the better.

As a jujutsu sorcerer and an active member of society, the opportunity to unwind away from his colleagues was indispensable. It would be like ventilation for the soul. Without fresh air, he got depressed. The key to working for extended periods of time was taking breathers when appropriate. That was the way he saw it, so he wasn't pleased to discover that a more experienced sorcerer would be accompanying him on this business trip. The fact that it was Satoru Gojo made his head hurt.

"Nanami, how about a quiz about Hokkaido?"

"No, feel free to do that on your own."

"Here's the first question," Gojo said. "My favorite sweet from Hokkaido is the famous *sanporoku* Baumkuchen!"

"Try again when you know what a quiz is."

"Okay, then let's play the buttered potatoes game. The rules are simple. The one who likes buttered potatoes the most wins. And

Resurrection Doll

I win! In all of Japan, there's only one person who likes buttered potatoes more than me, and it isn't you!"

"Who then?" Nanami said.

"Chiharu Matsuyama."

"You lie more often than you breathe."

"It cuts down on carbon dioxide emissions, no?"

"The amount of CO_2 from my sighs cancels it out," Nanami said. "Two men—two *sorcerers*—coming all the way to Hokkaido together is kind of sad."

"It's all right! It's like we're on a variety show."

"What variety show could be this annoying?"

The expressions on their faces couldn't have been more different as the two sorcerers walked down bustling Odori Avenue. Like Kyoto, Sapporo's layout was like a *go* board; as long as you followed the signs, you couldn't get lost. Getting the hang of the one-way streets was tricky, but at least sightseeing on foot in the Central Ward was convenient, and checking their location on a map was easy.

"Well, it's not like everything, as in *everything,* is in a grid. But it isn't hard to plot a route from one spot to another." As he spoke, Gojo produced a folded pamphlet. He opened it, revealing a simplified and easy-to-read map of the Central Ward, marked with several red circles.

"What's with the map?"

"Huh, huh, huh, Nanami?! Huh, huh, huh? Huh?"

"That's *really* annoying."

"Get your act together, man," Gojo said. "Think about it, what *else* could this be but Satoru Gojo's map of sweets?!"

"Feel free to do *that* on your own too."

"I try to conduct myself like a mentor, but you just don't look up to me."

"Because you've never been someone worth looking up to!" Nanami said.

Nanami sighed so hard his lungs seemed ready to collapse. In personal conversations with Gojo, 90 percent of the things out of the sorcerer's mouth were nonsense. Gojo could only ever only talk on his own wavelength. Responding in earnest was exhausting, but just letting him ramble on was irritating.

Gojo outranked him, was senior to him, and far surpassed him in strength and skill. Those who knew him well understood the significant inner distress this caused Nanami. For someone like Ijichi, this imbalance would likely have been an explosive problem.

"Anyway, why did you come with me?" Nanami asked. "This situation doesn't require two sorcerers, so—"

"So the incredibly handsome and strongest known sorcerer Satoru Gojo doesn't need to put in an appearance, right?"

Nanami's nerves were fraying, so he ignored that comment. But Gojo kept talking.

"I agree there's nothing to worry about. It's a solo investigation, and you're fully capable of handling it."

"Then why did you come?"

"To turn a simple job into an *utterly* simple job," Gojo said. "One person may be enough for the situation, and a grade 1 sorcerer at that, right? But I've heard a nasty curse user or something of the sort could be involved."

"You're saying we're up against a curse user equal to a grade 1 or special grade?"

"It's just a possibility."

"You aren't the kind of person who would come all the way here for a mere possibility," Nanami said.

"Your perceptiveness is striking. Oh, well. That's enough for now, isn't it? Maybe I'm just tired from my busy lifestyle and need a vacation up north."

"You can say that, but it's not true."

"Hey, Nanami. Look over there."

"Listen to me when I'm talking to you! Though I doubt anything I say matters," Nanami said, but he looked to where Gojo was pointing.

A bright yellow sign proclaimed BUTTERED POTATOES in massive red letters. The demand for attention couldn't have been more blaring.

"Now that I think about it, buttered-potato vendors really do adopt a bold style. But they only sell baked potatoes with butter, which aren't so hard to make at home," Gojo said.

"They're not all that different from stone-baked sweet potatoes."

"Now that you mention it, yes! You never fail to impress, Nanami! You see right behind the sunglasses!"

"Which only reveals where the eyes are."

"By the way, Nanami, we call potatoes *jagaimo* in Japanese. The *imo* means "potato," but where did the *jaga* come from?"

"According to one theory, potatoes entered Japan from a port in Jakarta," Nanami said.

"How did you know that off the top of your head?! Sometimes you scare me, Nanami."

"Why didn't *you* know that? You're Japan's second-ranked lover of buttered potatoes, aren't you?"

"Well, second is merely second. Only first is worth aiming for. Anyway... Greetings, good sir! An order of buttered potatoes, please!"

As they were talking, Gojo had slyly drawn near the vendor, so it was too late for Nanami to take preventive action.

"You're going to *eat*?" Nanami said.

"Yeah! After all, I'm the guy who loves buttered potatoes second most in Japan."

"But we came here to *work*."

"Then don't eat. I'll savor Hokkaido's cuisine on my own," Gojo said.

"No, I'll have some too."

"Thought so!"

The two men sat on a bench in Odori Park. One was dressed casually in black, the other in a formal suit. They both wore sunglasses. Sitting side by side, they munched their buttered potatoes. Sapporo is the kind of city where it's not unusual to see all sorts of performers and cosplayers out and about, but even so,

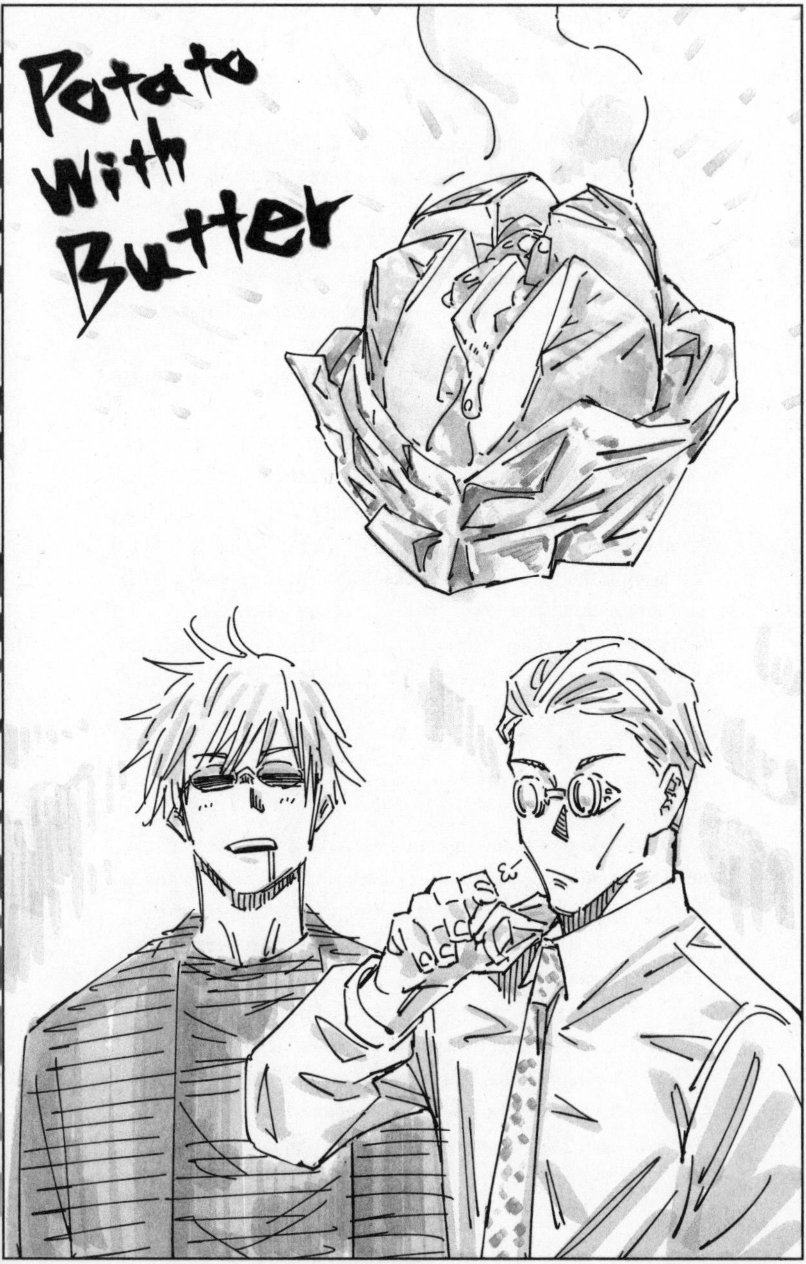
Potato with Butter

the antics of the pair sitting on the bench attracted the attention of passersby.

Nanami couldn't suppress his shock at the quality of their snack. "Wow, this is delicious! And steaming hot!"

"It wouldn't taste this good homemade!" Gojo cried out.

"Agreed! I totally underestimated buttered potatoes! There's a reason for having them grilled on the street after all!"

"It makes me want a beer. We should have done this after work."

"Beer? I don't get the desire to pair alcohol with something else that tastes good on its own," Nanami replied, disparagingly. "Hm? *Huh?*"

"What's wrong?"

"Your buttered potato looks different than mine."

"That's the *shiokara*. It tastes awesome," boasted Gojo, "and I'm not sharing."

"Well, I don't want any! It looks like a cursed spirit I vanquished the other day."

Nanami had come to Hokkaido hoping for a refreshing change of pace, but instead his stress was mounting.

After indulging in steaming-hot buttered potatoes, the two cleaned up their mess like responsible adults and began walking east through Odori Park toward the Sapporo TV Tower, where the park ends and a large street runs north to south near the bus center. The street is broad enough that a person might mistake it for the main artery of the city. Few pedestrians use it, though, perhaps because of the city's general layout.

"So what kind of vicious curse user are you investigating?" Gojo asked. "Not that we know there even *is* one."

"You came along even though you don't know?"

"Well, you're the one who has to handle it."

"Then you really shouldn't have come!" Nanami said. "Anyway, we just stuffed ourselves. How can you be eating an ice cream?!"

"You're eating one too."

Gojo was walking in front of Nanami as if that was where he belonged, carefully licking a cheese-and-milk twist ice cream so it wouldn't melt over the edge of the cone. He wasn't behaving at all like someone who didn't know anything about this mission, including which direction they should be heading.

Gojo said he couldn't understand Nanami's mundane choice of flavor—cookies-and-cream, not milk, or even chocolate—after they had come all the way to Hokkaido, adding that he couldn't bear the sight of it. Nanami glared at him through his sunglasses.

Nanami wanted to tell Gojo not to go marching ahead with no purpose, but he decided it would be faster to just explain the mission.

Normally, Gojo would have known about the mission and wouldn't have to ask Nanami. The fact that he did meant that he hadn't gotten any info beforehand. In other words, Gojo had known this mission wasn't important enough for his participation, but he had come along anyway. Nanami knew Gojo was busy and wouldn't come to the north country just to kill time. He wondered what Gojo's real purpose was. In any case, the only way to get him to reveal his true intention here was to solve the "doll disturbance" that he'd been briefed on earlier as quickly as possible. He decided a short explanation would be most efficient.

"It all started with a website called Yomotsu Hirasaka," Nanami began.

"That's quite a name, what with the reference to the realm between life and death."

"It's on an independent server to avoid search engines, but Ijichi was able to track it down."

"The man's got skills." Gojo's matter-of-fact tone suggested he expected nothing less.

Hearing that, Nanami guessed that Gojo had badgered Ijichi for Nanami's destination.

Kiyotaka Ijichi may not have been a superhacker, but once he knew what he was hunting for, he could figure out a way to find it. In this information-saturated society, many situations call for skill in searching rather than specialized knowledge. In that respect, Ijichi was of immense value.

That didn't mean, however, that Nanami could overlook the fact that he'd leaked information. He decided to have a few words with the man later.

"So what's the purpose of this website with the tasteless name?" Gojo asked. "Surely not charming videos."

"It's actually a pretty plain website, enough to make you nostalgic."

"You mean like there's a visitor counter at the top, and when it hits a certain number, you notify the administrator?"

"Sort of like that," Nanami replied.

"That does bring back memories, unfortunately."

"Yeah, we're getting old." Nanami took a bite of his cone, swallowed, and continued. "It turns out the site is a way to contact a curse user."

"How so?"

"There's a simple form. You fill in your request and send it. Then it displays the address to mail your payment to, and that's how you buy the product."

"Mail order? How analogue."

"The address can be traced to a property in Hokkaido owned by a small real estate agency. Apparently, it's a share house with a single room that's only the size of two tatami mats.

"That isn't enough room *to* share!" Gojo said.

"But the online form will randomly display one of twenty different P.O. boxes, which suggests something shady is going on," Nanami explained.

"The yakuza use fronts like that, but a curse user wouldn't think of it."

"For better or worse, a curse user with a venerable lineage would be unlikely to come up with such a system."

"So what does the website sell?" Gojo asked. "A rogue curse user could be charging for cursed tools to exorcize fly heads or taking orders to curse people. But I guess something of that scale wouldn't be enough to warrant bringing you in."

"You guess correctly," Nanami said.

"Think about who you're talking to. The higher-ups assigned you to the job and didn't fill me in, which means those geezers want to keep it a secret!"

"In that case, haven't you considered that they may have forbidden me from telling you?"

"Doesn't matter. If I wanted, I could make you talk. The most they can do is ask you *try* not to let me find out. But now that I'm here, it's too late for that," Gojo said.

"If you're so smart, you should find things out for yourself instead of asking me to explain everything."

"It's faster to ask junior sorcerers to do things that are a pain in the ass but not impossible," Gojo responded matter-of-factly.

Nanami sighed. He could only marvel at this more senior sorcerer who acted so high-and-mighty. Finally, he said, "Resurrections of the dead."

"Say what?"

Gojo didn't often doubt his ears, But what Nanami had said was ridiculous.

"The website advertises 'new vessels' called 'resurrection dolls' for summoning the souls of the dead," Nanami said.

"Sounds like a bad joke."

"It's most likely a fake, but…" Nanami trailed off.

"Okay, got it." Gojo waved his hand. During this short exchange, he had comprehended the situation and found it dispiriting. "Even if it's 99 percent likely to be nonsense, that still leaves a small chance that it's true. So ignoring it isn't an option."

The world is full of phenomena that don't require a second thought: morning follows night, ice is cold, and apples fall from trees. The world works because certain simple rules are so reliable it's almost funny. But if you overturn those rules, the world falls apart; if one plus one doesn't equal two, every other calculation fails, and if morning doesn't follow night the world could end. Laughably simple truths aren't funny if they stop being true. One of those truths is the irreversibility of time. It's no use crying over spilt milk. Regret solves nothing. You can't turn back time.

One of those phenomena so instinctively easy to understand is death.

"Those scumbags intent on burying Sukuna's vessel... They wanna keep me in the dark, huh?" Gojo said.

"So you understand."

"They misjudge me. Do they really think I'd rely on something like this?"

"If there's any chance at all, even if it's less than 1 percent, they'll crush it," Nanami explained. "That's why the powers that be continue to reign as the powers that be."

"I'm 100 percent sure these dolls are fake, though," Gojo said.

"Probably. If someone could raise the dead..."

"If someone could raise the dead, the world as we know it would have already ended."

The dead don't come back to life, so instead of dwelling on the past, people live the best they can before death. If coming back were possible, it would be a horrible curse upon the world.

One could call it the king of curses—the absolute curse.

"Well, this shady business only claims to raise babies," Nanami said. "So its plausibility is even more questionable."

"*Babies*? Say what?!"

"The business only allows customers to raise babies. I'm here to look into it."

"Even though the claim of resurrecting the dead is itself highly dubious," Gojo said.

"That doesn't mean I can just let it go. Work is work."

Gojo looked up as he nibbled on his cone. Ice cream had dripped on his thumb, and he licked it off. The expression on his face as he peered at Nanami through his sunglasses was one of exhaustion.

"Hey, Nanami? Was being a salaryman crappier than being a sorcerer?"

"Aside from whether one is cut out for it or not, there's little difference."

"Then our society is cursed," Gojo said.

"You make it sound hopeless."

"Whoever's selling those dolls—let's call them the Doll Maker—you know where they are, right? Which way do we go?"

"We already passed it. Because somebody walks wherever it suits him," Nanami said meaningfully.

"Huh? So it's my fault?"

"You're starting to make me think that being a salaryman was better because at least it didn't involve *you*."

Nanami couldn't help reconsidering his course in life.

Cities don't only expand laterally. When cities achieve maximum density on the surface, they usually start expanding vertically. In other words, buildings are stacked up high or dug deep underground.

"Oh, I get it. An underground city," said Gojo.

"I'm glad there are lots of entrances from the surface leading underground, but we sure took the long way," Nanami grumbled.

A sizeable rail network tends to be part of the underground footprint of a big city. The underground passage beginning at Sapporo Station is relatively new and spacious, and it affords access to a variety of major facilities all the way to Susukino. It explains why pedestrians are sparse aboveground despite the wide streets. The vast underground space, free of traffic signals and weather conditions, is like a separate city placed below the city above.

"Pretty fancy! We're underground, but there's a skylight!" Gojo marveled.

"There are convenience stores, bookstores, terraces, library kiosks, hair salons, and fortune-tellers! Along with all that, there might just be a Doll Maker too."

"Shouldn't we have started by coming down here?"

"I wanted to," Nanami said. "But *someone* insisted on chowing down on buttered potatoes first."

Gojo smirked. "Seriously? If I see that person, I'll give him a warning."

"Try the bathroom mirror."

"In any case, this place really is impressive. There are exhibition spaces, events, and performers. There's more human activity down here than on the surface." Gojo knitted his brows. "That isn't necessarily a good thing."

Sapporo is a distinctive city. Its people are diverse. In Tokyo, each district—Shibuya, Asakusa, Shinjuku, Akihabara, and so on—has its own characteristics, and people tend to gather in districts according to their personalities, which has given rise to terms like "the Shibuya type" and "the Akiba type." Sapporo, however, is a jumble. Youth gather in the shopping centers, nerds hit up shops selling anime swag, rickety shops line the shopping arcade, and the red-light district is a maelstrom of adult desires. These all mix in close proximity to one another, sometimes on opposite sides of the same road.

Of course, that meant a mixture of human emotions also congregated there: resentment, jealousy, anger, discrimination, obsession, envy, hatred, greed. In other cities, negative emotions would sort into different districts just as people do, but in Sapporo, there are no such distinctions.

Then there's the underground passage, a long tunnel and a vast underground space. Designed for convenience, that tube that connects most of the city's main facilities crowds together and carries along a wide variety of people and their negative emotions as they go to board their trains.

At first glance, this subterranean area seems full of life and impressive to behold, but to the sorcerers it looked like a crucible of the human spirit.

"This place makes the job easy. You could practically just follow your nose," remarked Gojo.

"Yes. Something feels obviously wrong."

The air in this underground city, with its immense amount of human traffic, was stagnant. The dismal aura was distinct. A sorcerer capable of following a cursed spirit merely from the residuals of its cursed technique would find this easier than tracing the source of a gas leak.

Nanami and Gojo threaded through the shifting crowds as they tracked the aura south. After ten minutes, they reached the end of the new, fashionable area and stepped into an older area with a much different appearance. The layout was convoluted, with side passages and subway yards. But instead of the crowd thinning out, congestion worsened. And somewhere amidst all those people coming and going...

Within this river of people was a zone that was...*stagnant*.

"Um, Nanami?"

"Yeah. There it is."

The two sorcerers were looking at a mother holding a baby. A boy of about five or six stood at her side.

As they drew near cautiously, Gojo and Nanami listened closely to the mother and son's conversation.

"Akito! Can't you understand?!"

"No, Mom! Stop carrying it! I don't like it!"

"You're a big brother now, so stop being selfish," the mother reprimanded. "Look what you've done... Natsuki is crying!"

"No, no, no! I'm not a big brother!"

The mother looked vexed as she shifted the baby Natsuki in her arms.

Of course, she *did* care about the boy named Akito, but an infant demands a parent's attention. And the woman was deeply attentive to it. Her face as she cradled the tiny form radiated a love so intense it bordered on insanity.

She was at a loss for how to handle her fussy son while consoling the baby. The average person wouldn't have noticed anything unusual, and might even find the scene charming. A young boy felt that the new arrival was dominating his mother's affections, so he was throwing a fit. Most adults would see the situation as amusing and commonplace.

But the boy named Akito was too distraught for the sorcerers to write this off as a mere tantrum.

No doubt he felt like he had lost his mother's attention. However, his animosity toward his younger brother was excessively harsh. The mother herself probably knew that, but her initial attempt to weather the tantrum with an uncomfortable smile turned to embarrassment, exhaustion, and anger.

"How can you say such a thing?!" she demanded.

"Because it's true!" said the boy.

"This is your little brother! You mustn't be mean!"

"That's *not* my little brother!"

"Akito!"

Enraged, the mother gave in to her emotion and swung her arm to slap her son. But the painful sound of her hand striking the child never came. Nanami had grabbed her wrist.

She gaped at him. "W-what are you doing?!"

The mother's confusion was understandable. From her point of view, Nanami and Gojo were suspicious individuals who were intruding.

She knew that physical punishment was wrong, but she hadn't been able to stop herself from lashing out over her son's comment about the infant, and the intervention of complete strangers was unacceptable.

However, Nanami and Gojo had reason to step in—as concerned citizens *and* as sorcerers.

"Let go of me!" the woman cried. "This is none of your business!"

"Actually, it *is*," Nanami said. "Do you know what it is you're holding?"

"What...?"

"Oh, I get it. This is what the dolls are." It finally dawned on Gojo. "*Agh!*"

Gojo was leaning in to peer at the baby in the mother's arms. "I wondered what we'd find...and there it is." He looked up at Nanami. "Selling such a thing and calling it a resurrection of the dead is the height of fraudulence!"

"S-stop it! Don't touch Natsuki!"

"Huh? Is that thing really so important? More than the child crying at your feet?" Gojo asked.

"Of course! I gave birth to this one too!"

"No, you *bought* it, right?" Nanami said.

At his words, the mother froze. Then she shuddered with a despair as intense as if he had forced his bare hand into her innards and grabbed her spine.

It was clear from what Nanami said that he knew what she had done.

"Cursed corpse?" The mother repeated Nanami's words, puzzled. Her intonation was awkward. She seemed unfamiliar with the term.

"Yes. That's what this thing is, simply put. Would it be easier to understand if I called it a *cursed doll*?"

Nanami was trying to be considerate toward someone who had no knowledge of sorcery. Gojo silently applauded Nanami for paying attention to such details based on his experience as a regular member of society.

"Doll? But look how real it is!" the mother cried out.

"It is astonishingly well-made. A normal person wouldn't be able to tell the difference between that and a real baby."

"But this baby *is* real!" she insisted.

"You made the transaction, so you know better than anyone that it *isn't*," Nanami said. "Not many sorcerers could make a cursed doll that is so lifelike. I'm just speculating, but I bet you had to pay with something other than money."

"*Ulp...*"

The baby in her arms was indeed well crafted. It wiggled its arms and legs as its pink cheeks trembled. It was a textbook example of all the traits that would awaken motherly instincts. But that was merely how it appeared to most people.

To a sorcerer's eyes, it was hideous.

"By any chance..." Nanami began.

Gojo cut him off. "I bet you had to fork over the corpse of the brat you wanted to revive."

"Gojo!"

"The business only works with babies because people have a hard time hefting adult bodies," Gojo said.

Nanami had planned to choose his words more circumspectly, so Gojo's bluntness was disappointing.

Judging from the mother's shock, however, Gojo had guessed correctly. The cursed corpse looked like it had in life because it consisted of real remains.

Someone who understood sorcery would know that such dolls were a perversion and an insult to sorcery, one that would have a corrupting influence on humans. However, the human semblance was enough to deceive the average person with the sentimental nightmare of reviving the dead.

Awaking from that nightmare required the truth, which Gojo dumped over her like freezing water. It would have been nice to think Gojo had deliberately volunteered to take on that task in order to spare Nanami, but Nanami knew how unlikely it was that Gojo would actually show such consideration.

Gojo continued. "It *looks* alive, but actually it's nothing but a pet robot, moving according to a program."

"You're lying!" cried the mother. "I heard about it! I heard that Natsuki could be brought back, and I paid the money!"

"As his mom, you should be able to tell from his little habits and facial expressions. That baby doesn't give a sense of having a living soul," said Nanami.

"Ah..." The mother faltered.

"Besides..."

Through his sunglasses, Nanami looked at the boy called Akito. He appeared to be about five or six and was clutching his mother's legs. He was worried, but he looked up at his mother's face with an expression of determination.

"Your son, at least, has noticed that something dark is trying to steal his mother."

"You don't understand..."

"Each person has their own form of truth. If the truth you want to choose is a present moment in which you haven't lost a child, I have no right to object to that." Nanami pushed up his sunglasses and waited a moment.

There were times when children exhibited a stronger will than adults expected from them. Akito knew he needed to do something to save his mother. Nanami admired that, even if it hurt him to see a small child having to face such a harsh reality.

So, with a quiet prayer, Nanami made his point. "The fact of the matter is that you're turning away from a present moment in which your living child is worried about you."

"Oh!"

In her heart, the mother understood. She understood that Nanami was correct and that she was avoiding reality. Nanami could see that, even if she didn't come right out and say it.

She had regained what she had lost, only to lose it again. Nanami knew how cruel that was, but he had to present her options.

"Dispelling human attachment is harder than expelling curses."

Gojo's comment referred to the tears and sobs that resulted from their confiscation of the cursed corpse.

From underground they couldn't see it, but the sun must have sunk toward the horizon. If they had used force, the wound in the woman's heart might have never healed, so their only choice had been to wait until she was ready to relinquish the doll herself.

Gojo had balked when Nanami told him he could at least carry something if he wasn't going to do any other work, but then he took the bag from Nanami. Inside was the cursed corpse they had taken from the mother.

"Nanami, this bag is too heavy," Gojo complained.

"Well, we can't just toss it. Besides, that doll is an important lead. If we compare the cursed energy in it to residuals, however faint, they'll point us in the general direction."

"I guess so. It seems the curse user who sold this thing intended to hide all traces, but yeah, it's fake. He's really careless."

As expected, they found the curse user's hideout easily.

It was in a very old part of the underground city. They had turned down a path branching away from the open area of the street and leading to the basement floor of a building, then zigzagged in a complicated way behind some stairs.

They found themselves in a space that might once have been an illegitimate drinking establishment. Such a poor location wasn't suited to a legitimate business but would have been perfect for something dodgy. It was hidden from human eyes with a cursed technique that used the same principle as a curtain. Nanami and Gojo had followed the residuals, and the traces were as easily detected as an unbroken trail of footsteps.

"I can tell this guy is short on help. It's strange that a third-rate curse user could establish a base so boldly without anyone bringing down the hammer," Gojo commented.

"Cursed spirits concentrate in cities, and sorcerers distribute their activities accordingly, which inevitably leads to neglect of the outlying areas."

"We could just let a seedy curse user like this go without it causing any major problem," speculated Gojo, "But the seller preyed upon that poor woman."

"So *we* gotta bring down the hammer."

Together, they kicked in the curse user's door. The wood and hinges screeched, and dust flew. The two sorcerers made a rude entrance worthy of a yakuza movie.

The one they'd taken to calling the Doll Maker shot to his feet.

"Wh-who're you?"

"If we look like customers, you need an optometrist, bottom-feeder!" Gojo said.

"We're sorcerers. *Proper* ones."

"Unlike *you*." Gojo's tone bore an unusual degree of contempt.

The room they had just barged into gave a new meaning to the word *tacky*. The interior decor was heavy-handed and indiscriminate; it was impossible to tell whether the theme was Japanese, Chinese, or Korean. Fake mummies and a guardian lion. A viper in formaldehyde. A painted black mask resembling something that would be sold in a souvenir shop.

The attire of the room's master, the Doll Maker, topped it all.

His clothes, made of cheap fabric, were vaguely reminiscent of something an *onmyoji* or a Shinto priest might wear. In addition, he had wrapped himself, as if with bandages, in crude seals that could only have contained miniscule amounts of magic, if any at all.

He looked like he was wearing a costume. Everything about his appearance was an insult to real sorcerers. His clients might be regular people, but it was laughable to think he could fool them.

"Sorcerers? Oh, I s-s-see... Y-you're sorcerers too!"

"What do you mean, 'too'? Surely you don't count *yourself* among sorcerers!" Gojo exclaimed.

Nanami probably felt the same way. The crease in his forehead was deep, and it expressed a visceral hatred for the Doll Maker's existence and his crimes. He wasn't holding a weapon, but he took a stance that would allow him to engage in battle at any moment.

The Doll Maker was a fake sorcerer, but even a regular person would have found Nanami, a grade 1 sorcerer, intimidating. It would be foolish—or crazy—to take him lightly.

"Uh...uh...um... W-why are you here?" stammered the Doll Maker.

"If you don't know why we're here already, then just shut up. Playing dumb isn't cute," said Gojo

"I...I don't have any time! No time at all!"

"Neither do we. It's almost four o'clock. This may be a business trip, but we shouldn't be working outside of regular business hours," Nanami replied.

Nanami and Gojo advanced together toward the Doll Maker.

If the two stayed side by side and blocked the door of the cramped room, the Doll Maker would have nowhere to run. They had him cornered.

The Doll Maker didn't have many options. He could play it reckless and try to flee past the two sorcerers, he could put up a crude resistance by swinging a blunt object, or he could submit to capture.

In the end...the Doll Maker didn't choose any of these.

"H-h-h-h...help me!" he screamed.

"*Huh?*" Nanami and Gojo were taken off guard by this outburst.

"I...I-I-I...I'm...I'm so glad you're here!" The Doll Maker dropped to his knees and grabbed onto Nanami's legs. "I was actually going to look for you myself! For real sorcerers, I mean! Y-you gotta help me! If you want money, I have some saved up! So, please!"

That was when Nanami and Gojo noticed something wrong. The Doll Maker certainly wasn't worthy of being called a curse user. A single first-year student at Jujutsu High—never mind Nanami—could easily suppress him. That's how weak the Doll Maker was as a sorcerer or a curse user.

Too weak.

The cursed energy in the cursed corpse wasn't strong, and the cursed technique was simple, so the doll was no more than a sham that could respond mechanically to human prompts. The Doll Maker, however, was too weak even to have done that.

It was hard to imagine that the man before their eyes, the man clinging to Nanami's legs, was a curse user, even at a low level. Nonetheless, he was indeed emanating an amount of cursed energy equal to that of the cursed corpse.

Which led them to a specific conclusion.

"Nanami..." Gojo began.

Nanami understood. "We thought he was cursing people for sport, but it turns out he's a victim himself."

As if those comments served as a signal, a change occurred in the man. He ripped off the many seals wrapped around his clothes. Several arm-like appendages shot out from underneath, like whips.

Nanami made a small movement as though to dodge, with minimal movement, but suddenly changed tack.

As he moved, a few small bug-like creatures flew at him from the tips of the swinging arms. Evading their attacks, Nanami whipped off his suit jacket and used it to bat down the bug-like things.

The Doll Maker's body was transforming into a doll of flesh. Human and doll fused into a contorted mass. His neck and left arm retained some semblance of their original form, but the left side of his chest and below were horribly deformed. A doll's head, twisted in aggravation, was biting into his heart. Several wooden skeletal structures, sharp as bamboo spears, intersected and pierced his flesh as over 70 percent of his body transformed into a doll, giving him the silhouette of a spider.

"Aaaaaagh! Help, help! Money! Money! I've got money, so exorcize th-this! G-g-get th-this thing out of me!"

The Doll Maker was raving with pain and fear as the countless arms swung like whips. They had the force of storm winds, strong enough to pulverize bones. But the arms were nearly as frightening as the swarm of insects welling from inside his stomach and crawling over his skin.

No...

Looking more closely, Nanami realized that the countless bugs were in fact small cursed corpses. As they devoured the Doll Maker's body and the corpses of babies hidden under his clothes, they gradually grew and multiplied.

"A cursed corpse factory and self-generating cursed corpses?" Nanami said.

Even now, the cursed corpses were slowly reproducing as if weaving hair and flesh. There was no way to determine the degree to which they had devoured the man's body.

That answered the final question they had.

"I've been wondering what happened to the flesh left over after you used the skin from the corpses to make cursed dolls for the parents. Now I see you were using it to replace your own consumed flesh," said Gojo.

Nanami concurred: "I was also wondering how he made such sophisticated-looking cursed corpses."

"They aren't the kind of thing a modern-day curse user could just dash off," Gojo said. "He's probably the remnant of an old line of sorcerers who pulled a cursed tool out of storage...or found an unmanageable cursed object."

"So you established a complicated pay-by-mail system, at first probably just to rake in cash. That alone proves your dishonest motives. Claiming extenuating circumstances simply won't cut it," Nanami said to the Doll Maker, with a sigh that expressed immense exhaustion.

"That thing devours the living as well as the dead, so I bet you really had to keep your nose to the grindstone." As he said this, Gojo's shoulders slumped as if he had simply run out of energy.

A doll that feasted on human flesh to produce more dolls, and a Doll Maker who gathered dead bodies to replace his own consumed flesh. He couldn't keep up and eventually became possessed by that doll. None of it should have existed in this world.

Nanami and Gojo wore the same look on their faces. It expressed grim resignation.

They had accepted the harsh reality, and it didn't bode well for the Doll Maker wheedling for mercy.

"Huh? N-no! H-h-help me! P-please!" he begged.

"Huh? No can do. Surely you know that," Gojo said.

"If it hadn't gotten to this point already, Ieiri might have removed it, but..." Nanami reached behind his back, where a large hatchet-like blade was strapped.

This was the weapon he bore.

After abandoning his life as a salaryman, he had become a sorcerer and taken up this righteous weapon. Nanami pointed it at the Doll Maker.

"W-wait! What's that?!" the Doll Maker cried.

"Seven to three." Nanami flourished his blade. "My cursed technique divides my targets to forcibly create a weak spot at the ratio point of seven to three. That holds for both living things and non-living things. You're a fusion of both, so it'll treat you as a single object."

"W-what are you talking about?"

Nanami was divulging his cursed technique. This was part of a binding vow that allowed him to amplify his cursed technique's effect. Revealing information carried a disadvantage but also increased attack strength.

In other words, Nanami was announcing his desire for maximum damage.

"I do pity the state you're in, but from the start you were clearly using dangerous sorcery to make some dough," Nanami said.

"H-h-hey... You're kidding, right? I-I'm human! W-what would a s-sorcerer do against a human being w-with that blade?!"

"It's too late for you."

"No, no! No, no, no! *Ulp...* You can do that?! I brought the dead back to life! I offered comfort to the human heart! I *saved* them! Only *I* could do that! B-but now you're g-gonna k-k-k-kill me?!"

"You can barely talk, and you're losing control of your conscious self," replied Nanami. "And even worse..."

Nanami brandished his blade with precise control in the cramped space.

To the Doll Maker's eyes, his action was clearly full of murderous intent. With his back against the wall, there was little he could do. Fear and frustration seized him.

"This is because you scattered curses among other people, thereby making a curse of *yourself*," Nanami said.

Nanami's words cut the threads of the man's tension, which were already about to snap.

"I'll kill youuuuuuuuuuuuuuuuuuuuuuu..."

The Doll Maker flung himself at Nanami. He flailed his remaining human arm and countless other doll appendages.

Nanami didn't flinch. He uncoiled like a spring, parting the air with his blade. "Act like an adult and take responsibility for your actions."

One stroke.

"...uuuu!"

The Doll Maker never even released a final gasp.

The cursed technique, amplified by revealing information, segmented the Doll Maker's body at precisely the ratio of seven to three. Nanami struck downward at an angle from the shoulder, exactly between the human and doll-like parts, which then flopped to the floor.

The severed doll body, which had probably been feeding on the Doll Maker's soul, beat out an inorganic, rattling clamor and eventually fell still.

With faint sounds that didn't form words, the Doll Maker stopped moving, like a doll with severed strings. Then, as if a cord had been severed, the small bug-like cursed corpses stopped moving, one after the other.

Perhaps the flesh and blood, the unchanged portion that Nanami had severed from the doll, was able at the last moment to die a human death.

Nanami's single strike had returned the man's humanity, though it was a relief for no one.

"Well done, Nanami."

Gojo slapped him on the shoulder, and Nanami swung his arms in circles as if to work out the kinks.

"It would've been easier if you had done it," Nanami said.

"But your cursed technique was more suited to giving him a human death."

"I don't *want* to be suited to that kind of job."

"For now, let's lower the curtain and request a clean-up. Handling stiffs isn't my area," Gojo said.

"You barely did anything this time!"

Nanami loosed a long sigh, and the room fell silent. The guardian lions, fake mummies, and vipers in formaldehyde remained enshrined in the room, which now had no master.

Had the room's former master been human? Or a doll? By the time the sorcerers arrived, that was unclear. However, the bright blood running across the floor seemed to prove he was human.

Eventually, that too was wiped away, as if nothing had ever happened.

In the end, only silence remained in that remote underground den.

"They say a good doctor follows his own advice."

Gojo had been silently swirling his drink for a while, and at first, Nanami didn't realize the instructor was speaking to him.

"Does this pertain to the Doll Maker?"

"No, to sorcerers in general," Gojo said. "Ultimately, handling curses is about handling negative human emotions. It involves a lot of depressing work."

"You're talking about the danger of building up a curse within oneself?" inquired Nanami.

"Even if you get used to this line of work, it doesn't feel good. Makes me wanna get drunk."

"You ordered a Florida, right? That's non-alcoholic," Nanami said.

"I didn't do anything, right? So I'm not the one who needs to get drunk." Gojo stated outright.

"Don't rub it in."

Gojo laughed as he watched Nanami drain his gimlet.

"Nanami, you're a little bit of a softy."

"Where did *that* come from?"

"You know how to shut stuff out when necessary, but you're not totally immune to it. Adults have ways of relieving the friction that creates. Like alcohol, the wonder drug," Gojo said.

"This isn't a pleasant conversation. Must we continue?"

"I'm not teasing you."

Doubtful, Nanami looked at Gojo through his sunglasses. Gojo, he noticed, wasn't wearing his customary smirk. Nanami said nothing.

"Humans give birth to curses, so the time will come when one of my students will face the ill will of somebody truly nasty," Gojo said.

"Because they're sorcerers."

The world was an unfair place. Human ill will bred curses. All people, not just sorcerers, were capable of steeping themselves in bitterness, giving up, and drowning in lost hopes. Nanami knew that. And Gojo knew that Nanami was a man with such a past.

"We have ways of removing the poison that has circulated to our hearts," Gojo said. "The young don't have that skill. They're too sensitive. At least once, that poison will break their hearts."

"I suppose it's the adults' job to handle the poison that affects the young. As a teacher, you understand that, right?"

"Yes, I do. That's why I came to talk to you."

Gojo drained his glass and placed another order with the bartender. "Two Cinderellas."

"You must be joking." Nanami was disbelieving.

An excessively sweet drink. It was, of course, non-alcoholic, basically just a mix of juices.

Gojo directed his eyes to the shelf behind the bar and continued speaking. "There's a kid I want to have you look after at some point."

"Is it Fushiguro?"

"Yuji Itadori. You know him."

"I heard he died." said Nanami.

"He harbors the King of Curses, which is a far cry from some charlatan using dolls to bring back the dead."

The bartender set two glasses on the counter. The liquid inside was amber, like the setting sun—though, given the drink's name, maybe of a *full moon* would be more apt. Or the color of the hair on the head of the boy they were discussing.

The cocktail was saccharine, like an overly romantic fairy tale in which everyone lives happily ever after.

Gojo lifted his glass and swirled its contents. "I'm busy, so this chance to kick back and talk to you without interruption is precious."

"I know you hate the jujutsu world at the moment, but I side with the regulations now. I don't know what you have in mind regarding Sukuna's vessel, but..."

"I don't mean Sukuna's vessel," Gojo said. "I'm talking about the kid named Yuji Itadori."

"His situation is not so simple that we can ignore the obvious when talking about him."

"Yuji's an all right kid." Gojo ran his finger around the rim of his glass. A faint, high sound, like that of a stringed instrument, rang out. "He's determined and brave. And he's decisive in a fight. Nonetheless, he's a bit too upright sometimes. I'm worried that it will break his heart eventually."

"Why are you telling me this?" Nanami asked.

"I told you. I'm busy, so I can't promise I'll be able to give him the necessary spiritual guidance. If I could hand him off to you sometime, it'd help."

"And you think I'll do you this favor?"

"That's why I'm asking. Whether he's a sorcerer or Sukuna's vessel, you're an adult who can help him grow up healthy." Gojo was always flippant, careless and half-joking, but that was precisely why you could tell when he was serious. "I need someone who understands the suffering people go through. Someone like you."

"Did you come all the way here to sweet-talk me?"

"Well, you know I have a taste for sweets." Laughing, Gojo tilted his glass toward Nanami.

The cocktail was sweet, sour, and glistening amber. Nanami stared at it in silence, as if it contained the precariousness of youth.

"I'm no good at that stuff," he said.

Without any conscious attempt to synchronize, the two drained their glasses as one.

"That's *sweet*!"

"Delicious, ain't it?"

Their voices resonated in the subdued bar.

The sorcerers' night grew long, and the sweet taste on their tongues was like all the swirling suffering of the world.

CHAPTER 3 Allegory in Darkness

It takes a forest to hide a tree.

So maybe it takes a city to hide a person.

If so, it makes sense that cursed spirits who were like people would establish their hideouts in a city. Cursed spirits might be more comfortable living in places full of fear, like deep in the mountains or in a dark, dense forest, where a human being would find it difficult to live. Nonetheless, cursed spirits plot the overthrow of modern society, so establishing bases in urban areas makes sense, whether they are on the offense or in retreat. And places where there are gatherings of negative emotions are best.

That's how everyone working at a certain fraudulent company ended up murdered.

"These kinds of guys are easy. They group up and make a nest away from prying eyes, so it's easy to wipe them out."

Jogo laughed, grinding the cinders beneath his feet.

Approximately two minutes before, there had been six people alive in this office.

He had considered various ways of dealing with them, but burning was fastest.

Mahito was poking at a gaudy vase on a shelf. "People used this building, right? If there's someone higher up, won't that be a problem?"

Jogo smiled reassuringly and was about to answer when an incomprehensible voice interrupted.

"ᄋᆰᅦᆌᆄᆵᄌᄟᄚ"

"Hey! No talking, Hanami! It makes my head itch!"

Hanami's words sounded like nothing but noise, but they somehow conveyed his will directly into one's head. Jogo found that unpleasant; it irritated him.

Jogo noticed Mahito looking at him.

Jogo's irritation was obvious as he explained. "*Hmph!* Don't worry! I asked Geto about our target. The bosses of these shady types usually know all about the prohibited stuff they're getting up to."

"So they'll understand it's the result of curses and stay away?"

"Exactly. This isn't the kind of place that upstanding people frequent. so it's a perfect hiding spot," Jogo said.

"You sure?"

"What's wrong, Mahito? Are you unsatisfied? What don't you like? It's a good location to prepare an attack on the city and to flee to if necessary."

"Uh...yeah, I guess so, but..."

"Yeah? Well, spit it out!!"

"The interior decor is really tasteless," Mahito said.

"*Hunh?!*" A small eruption came from Jogo's head with a *poof!* His single eye narrowed, forming a ridge like a mountain range on his brow.

"It's gaudy!" Mahito said. "Look at this shiny vase and golden lion! And this cheap sideboard!"

"What are you talking about?! I don't know what's gotten into you that you're being so picky these days!"

"It's the movies."

"Movies? You like movies? They're nothing but human superficialities," Jogo said.

"Actually, they're a reliable resource to study the soul," Mahito said, smiling. A human looking at him then might think he resembled an elementary school student puffed up with pride as he recited knowledge he'd acquired for a book report. "To be honest, it isn't a very interesting topic for me either, but I don't exactly dislike human visual aesthetics. Still, this room is too colorful. It hurts my eyes."

"Quit complaining like a spoiled brat," Jogo said. "We can burn or throw away anything we don't like."

"No, I'm going to find my own place where I can relax."

"What? Hey! Where are you going?!"

Ignoring Jogo's protests, Mahito waved his hand over his back and disappeared, like smoke or wind.

"*Urgh...* Maybe it's because human fear created him, but he's too frivolous, even for a curse. Movies, of all things!"

As he grumbled, Jogo removed a pipe from his pocket and tucked it in his mouth.

It didn't look like a normal pipe. It resembled a face, and it screamed when he sucked through it.

"Drat that Mahito!"

Jogo swiveled his eye to survey the room.

"Now this place looks tasteless to *me* too!"

"誡解洗焰"

"I said shut up!!"

Mahito would have to find a suitable hideout for himself.

As he strolled around town, he alternated turning left or right each time he came upon a traffic signal, he followed cats prancing along ahead of him, and he walked in the direction of clouds whose shapes struck his fancy. As he did so, he felt keenly how humorous humans were. The city belonged to them, but none of the humans passing through the streets walked as freely as Mahito. Everyone looked tense, bound by inhibitions and vanity, living shortsighted lives in a vast and fathomless city.

Without ever knowing how infinitely large the sky was, they took a city of stone they had divided up, further divided it as their souls saw fit, and lived subserviently within those narrow confines.

Mahito had come to understand their worldview through the words they used. For example, they called *this* "morality," and they called *that* "common sense," and they called *that* "emotion." Their souls received external stimuli and they merely metabolized them, like machines. This process controlled their bodies, so they feared the judgment of others, sought the world's favor, and relinquished their freedom.

"What a waste."

The fetters of affectation, a human creation, bound them all.

This was why curses had to change human beings. If all they could do was crawl around clumsily like that, they should surrender their world to others.

That's what Mahito thought.

Think as your soul desires. Walk where the wind blows.

The sun would soon sink in the west. He could hear a river murmuring.

"This isn't bad."

The hideout Mahito found was under a large bridge that crossed over a river. It was a tunnel as wide open at each end as a Buddhist temple. What looked like plumbing passed through the tunnel, and clear water ran toward the river. He suspected it was purified wastewater, so it didn't bother him. The air was damp, and he smelled a vegetative odor, like moss, but the tunnel was spacious enough to bound around, and the cool feeling of concrete was refreshing.

Cursed spirits like certain seasons. Negative emotions accumulate in humans from the end of winter toward the spring. They reach peak maturity during the rainy season. Inside the moist tunnel, the air was humid like in the rainy season. The dim light was gloomy, which was perfect for breeding fear, and the damp was comfortable.

"Yes, this will do nicely."

Following one's instincts is the best way to choose a place to live.

It is probably what's best for humans too, but while they never did it intuitively, Mahito was able to decide without hesitation. Drifting was freedom, and so was feeling at ease.

In high spirits, he strode across the concrete floor, his footsteps ringing out on the hard surface.

He was thinking about how smoothly the metabolizing of souls would go in this welcoming atmosphere when he noticed the presence of...something.

"Hm?"

At first glance, it didn't appear to be anything more than a bundle of old rags. He thought he was looking at trash, the result of humans and their littering. With the silhouette of a large draw-string sack slumped leaning against the wall, it was motionless. As he looked at it, though, Mahito realized it had the shape of a soul.

Oh, so it's alive.

It was a man wrapped in an old cloth. His long hair and beard had obscured his human shape. His exact age wasn't readily apparent. He might have been sixty or over eighty—elderly, at any rate.

His presence was a nuisance. Mahito had finally found a hideout, and someone was already living there. Of course, it would be no trouble getting rid of the man, but still, it was unpleasant, like noticing a stain on the wall of a new house.

Mahito released a small sigh and extended his hand toward the old man.

Suddenly, the man spoke.

"Sorry if you find me unpleasant."

"Huh?"

"I don't know what you've come for, but finding an old-timer like me here must have spoiled your mood. But I don't have anywhere else to go either."

Mahito was taken aback.

The old man was clearly aware of Mahito and addressing him. That wouldn't be surprising if they had both been human, but Mahito was a cursed spirit. The eyes of a mere human shouldn't be capable of apprehending the existence of cursed spirits.

Of course, it wasn't *impossible*. Humans with innate cursed energy could perceive cursed spirits, and that wasn't exactly rare.

What drew Mahito's interest further was the fact that the old man didn't have any *eyes*. Horrible burn scars covered the sockets where his eyes should have been.

Even sorcerers looked at the world through their eyes. In addition to being aware, sorcerers relied on vision. For that reason, most sorcerers used sunglasses to hide where they were looking. They did it to avoid arousing suspicion in cursed spirits, as well as to preserve their emotional equilibrium in a world teeming with curses.

But this old man wasn't like that.

"You can see me?"

The old man nodded in response to Mahito's question. "I can *sense* you."

"Even though you can't even see your surroundings?"

"Of course. Like the scenery, it's unclear to me what kind of features you have, what color your skin is, and whether you're a man or a woman," said the old man. "Nonetheless, I know you're there."

"Are you a sorcerer?" Mahito asked.

"I don't think so."

"You don't sound sure. Even though you're referring to yourself."

"I've been unsure about myself for a long time," the man responded.

Mahito noticed something odd, then. He usually sensed the souls of human beings as shapes: they could be spiky, shriveled, weak, or quivering as if reverberating. They fluctuated. However, this old man's soul revealed little fluctuation. He was like a grassy field with no wind, a sea with no waves, a blue sky with no clouds.

No, Mahito realized. The more appropriate comparison was to a rock.

He had a soul like a boulder by the side of the road. Unadorned, unpolished, unmoving, unwavering. It just passed the time in tranquility, quietly gathering moss.

That was the shape of the old man's soul.

No matter how mild human beings might be, no matter how old they got, their souls wavered. Even after the passage of years, preconceptions didn't vanish entirely and people found it hard to dispel their greed and conquer their fears.

But the old man was different.

His soul was peaceful. He had fully accepted that he would wither with time, and that was why he wouldn't waste his life in unnecessary distress. It was almost like a truly natural existence.

Mahito had never encountered a human being like that before.

The tunnel became Mahito's temporary nest.

He brought in a hammock he'd found and hung it from the tunnel's pipes, lounged in it, and passed the time engaged in activities like reading. He'd gotten the idea from a movie he'd once seen about a castaway on a desert island. The castaway had reclaimed a measure of ease by erecting a hammock. It looked comfortable, so Mahito tried it and found he liked it.

The city's noise didn't quite reach the interior of the tunnel, leaving only a vague susurration that Mahito rather enjoyed. The tunnel was a good environment for peace and quiet.

As Mahito relaxed and acquired knowledge from the books he read, he would sometimes stare at the ceiling or look down at the old man sitting in the corner, whose position and expression rarely seemed to change.

"How do you survive?" Mahito asked. "I don't get it."

Mahito had decided not to kill the old man. The old man didn't get in his way. He was quieter than a stray cat and only ever sat there, cooling his heels. If his presence or absence made no difference, then why bother getting rid of him?

Mahito had once heard the expression "Man is the thinking reed." He liked the humorous way it expressed human frailty through a comparison to weeds, as well as the way it turned the human soul's captivity to reason into a point of pride.

But the old man was a reed that *didn't* think. Actually, he was so silent and motionless that he was more like moss. The old man was just there, never speaking.

Sometimes Mahito would notice that the old man had gone missing from his spot; then, just as abruptly, he would back again, asleep in his corner. The man must have been eating somewhere, but he didn't appear to gain weight. If the typical body weight starts at 100 percent, when the man's dropped to 80 percent, he likely went somewhere to consume just enough to bump it back up to 100.

That manner of existence was incredibly instinctual, more like a natural phenomenon than a life.

"Maybe that's why you can see me," Mahito speculated absentmindedly.

He hadn't really been addressing the man, but when he spoke those words to himself, it sounded like he was. When he noticed that his words didn't cause the slightest ruffle in the old man's soul, he decided to address him directly.

"How long have you been here?"

"Well, I suppose I've passed a few winters here, but I'm not certain," the old man answered with a quiet mutter.

Mahito felt that occasional conversation was only natural when two living things were sharing company, both with souls and aware of each other.

"Don't you get bored?"

Mahito spoke casually, and the old man responded in kind.

"I forgot *how* to be bored."

Mahito continued to question the man. "What do you do all the time?"

"Nothing. I just listen to the sounds."

"Sounds?"

"The sound of the flowing water," the man responded.

"Is that fun?"

"No. But I've forgotten how to have fun, so it doesn't bother me."

Mahito thought that made sense and nodded.

Maybe the old man's soul had worn away to the point that he didn't find boredom unpleasant. Or maybe his soul was less worn than *polished*. City people always wanted *more* and lamented discomfort. Momentary satisfaction only made them greedier, so they acquired negative emotions and their souls bloated. The old man's soul, on the other hand, was slim, even *stylish*.

Fattened souls, when satiated, gave birth to the fear of losing the satisfaction of the moment. Thus, they changed, and that produced curses.

"Do you—Come to think of it, you got a name?"

The old man stared into space for a moment. "I got rid of it. If you need to call me by a name, use whatever name you like."

"Are there humans without names? Even curses have names."

"I don't meet people, so I don't need a name."

"But you must have trouble without one," Mahito said.

"What would I need a name for?"

"For your grave."

"I don't need a grave with my name on it. They'll put me in a mass grave or I'll rot away where no one can find me and return to dust."

"Can't you understand a joke?" Mahito said.

"Oh, were you joking?"

The old man didn't laugh and neither did Mahito.

Mahito sensed a youthfulness behind the man's aged exterior.

Perhaps an innocent personality, purified through his lack of attachments, had made him younger than he looked.

Mahito's interest in the old man increased. He had never encountered a human being like this before and had never sensed a soul with this shape. The old man was a curious specimen to him.

What kind of life had he lived to turn out like *this*?

And how much fun would it be for Mahito to mess around with a soul like this? What mischief could he get up to with such a soul? What kind of curse would such an individual give rise to?

Intrigued, Mahito questioned the old man.

"Why are you here?"

"Why?"

The old man looked up at the ceiling through the hair that covered his face.

Scars obscured the place where his eyes had been. Mahito knew the old man couldn't see anything, but apparently when humans think, they turn their gaze upon empty space. Noticing that, one of Mahito's areas of curiosity was satisfied.

"Well, you weren't born and raised in this tunnel, were you? You're a human being, so you must have lived in that noisy city."

"Yes, that's right," the old man agreed, "Once upon a time, I led a busy life. I inherited a house, I worked, I saved money and cared for a family."

"So you had status."

"By society's standards, yes," said the old man. "When I think about it now, though, none of that meant much."

"Why did you start living like a rat in a hole in the ground?"

"Because I lost everything I had—my status, money, even a place to be."

"You *lost* it?" Mahito asked.

"I got swindled. That was when my eyes were burned and I lost all light."

Mahito remembered the company Jogo had attacked.

"Someone tricked you," Mahito said. "You must've been gullible."

"Well, I didn't mind the deception."

"You're a strange old man. You get your kicks out of being tricked?"

"Yes, because I was in a position that invited others to attempt to swindle me. It was an old friend and my wife who did it," the man explained without flinching. "They made the burning of my eyes look like an accident and claimed they had to take care of me. Then, before I knew it, they had stolen control over all my affairs."

"That's pretty harsh, but you talk about it like it happened to someone else."

"They were in love, but neither one loved *me*. And that hit harder than the actual deception."

Mahito had difficulty interpreting the old man's words.

Love. Was that really such an important thing? Human beings were obsessed with it, Mahito knew. Some curses came from love, and some of those were incredibly fearsome. However, Mahito didn't understand how the mechanism of human love was any different from a cat's attachment to its favorite blanket.

"Didn't you curse the people who tricked you?" he asked.

"Not particularly," the old man replied.

"Not particularly, huh? People in such circumstances usually get angry and bear a grudge. Then their souls degenerate."

"Yes, but I didn't even have the energy to seek revenge or to make them suffer."

"Oh, I see." Mahito nodded in understanding.

Whether he was able to imagine human emotions or not, Mahito had studied movies, novels, and poetry. By extrapolating from these samples, he was able to grasp the basics of what the old man was saying.

Mahito said, "In other words, you were in such distress that your soul approached death. You blew past grudges and curses and went straight to rock bottom."

The old man slowly shook his head. "Maybe I was hopeless, but you're talking about intense despair."

"Are they different?"

"Yes. They're all I've experienced."

The old man raised his face as if searching through his past.

"I didn't experience burning anger or dismal sadness. I think I was just tired. Work, acclaim, status, responsibility, social responsibilities, finances, fame... Those things were exhausting, so exhausting that they emptied me."

"And that's why you didn't get angry at the deception."

"It was a relief. They say hopelessness can actually make one feel lighter." The old man's voice had a cold clarity, like impure water that had passed through a filter. It sounded peaceful. "Light, money, love... I lost everything, so when I walked around town, suddenly everything had lost meaning. In that state, everything looked different."

"Even though you couldn't see?" Mahito asked.

"Yes. When you can't see, sounds stretch to infinity and there's only the wind. There aren't even any walls partitioning the city. There's just a limitless darkness, like a starless night sky. It was the first time I had experienced the world as an open space. And then I realized I was *free*."

Mahito blinked.

The old man's way of thinking was unlike anything Mahito had encountered in a human before. Even hearing of the old man's past, Mahito was unable to comprehend his way of thinking.

Yet he did appear truly free in Mahito's eyes. Even in this tunnel, the old man knew the sky was wide. He probably knew that better than all the people walking around town, no matter their status. Precisely because the old man—who looked like nothing more than an outcast and a straggler—had lost his wealth and social standing and every human connection, he had learned the meaning of the word *freedom*, and he was now living it.

Without attachment, without fear...without cursing. He simply existed. He simply lived.

"Not all those who wander are lost, huh?" Mahito said.

"Isn't that a bit depressing for a quote from Tolkien?"

Mahito smiled at how the old man had immediately identified the quote, one Mahito had read in a random book he'd picked up.

"Are you a big reader?" he asked the man.

"I read to gather information."

"A wide range of learning is a good thing."

Mahito had to wonder that if humans were creatures whose fear gave birth to curses, was this old man really a human being? His feelings at the moment were difficult to describe, but they were peaceful. Since encountering human beings, he had never felt such peace.

"If everyone in the human world was like you, I'd never have been born," Mahito noted.

He looked at the book in his hands. The old man fell silent and stared into space as he always did.

Humans gave birth to curses, but curses killed humans. There was no possibility of coexistence. Yet a curse and human were coexisting there in this tunnel.

The situation was unusual, but it was a serene time, and together they passed it in serenity.

As a matter of course, people hated and feared others.

They couldn't see souls, so they had to *imagine* how others felt. Furthermore, they were at the mercy of their own emotions. They merely reacted to stimuli, never recognizing the fluctuations in their own souls. They didn't even know where their souls were.

Mahito pondered the matter.

The blind old man had lost all light and all ties to other people, resulting in minimal stimulation to his soul. As a result, the unnecessary dross of the external world had stopped influencing him, so he spent more time facing inward.

"That's like the ascetic practice of a monk," Mahito muttered to himself. "Intense introspection, more time peering into your own soul."

As he walked along the street, Mahito skimmed a worn-out copy of the Heart Sutra. The scripture was like a textbook for controlling the soul. In their own way, people long ago had studied techniques for distinguishing the soul from substance.

Through his manner of living, the old man had unintentionally reached an enlightened state. Perhaps that was how he had learned to sense souls in the dark. That was the explanation Mahito came up with regarding the old man's detection of curses.

"He must have already had the potential. After all, it's easy for the talent to bloom in introverts."

If Mahito pondered the old man further, he might be able to guess the sorcerers' training methods and techniques for manifesting cursed energy. Then he might be able to turn talented human beings into sorcerers and curse users.

He might be able to spur a curse user he had groomed into becoming a sorcerer.

That would be an interesting experiment. It was easier to upset human souls by making them fight each other than by having them exorcize curses. And he doubted Sukuna's vessel was any exception.

However...

Maybe I'll save that for later.

Mahito mulled this over in a leisurely way.

He was free. He moved when he felt like moving and rested when he felt like resting. And at the moment, he didn't feel like putting any plans into action. For now, he would gather knowledge and lose himself in thought.

He had picked up a few more books, and he wanted to bask in the comfort of the quiet tunnel and read fantasy novels. His gait was light, and he even began humming as he walked with the flow of human traffic.

Then he heard loud voices coming from between the buildings.

"You really piss me off!"

Glancing in that direction, Mahito saw two young human beings: a skinny man with long hair and a well-built man with a shaved head. These types of people were usually described as "rough."

The man with long hair was grinning sheepishly as he listened to the angry man with the shaved head.

"It ain't funny! Every moron talks tough, but all they got is talk! Then they make excuses! I'd like to kill every last one of 'em!"

"Sure, but if you ever got, like, super angry, could you actually do it?" asked the long-haired man.

"Yeah! Killin' ain't nuthin'!"

"Fer real?"

Mahito's eyes narrowed as he listened.

He didn't mind honest impulses, but Mahito knew human beings like this were almost always all talk.

"Yeah, for real!" yelled the well-built man. "I'd snuff out *anyone*, dude!"

If so, he should shut up and do it.

Mahito thought about teaching the man what it felt like to kill, and he even started to reach out, but then he noticed the weight of the book in his hand and gave up the idea. Instead of messing around with these men, he wanted to hurry back to the comfort of the tunnel and get lost in a book.

"I'll really do it, dude!"

The shaven-headed man's words sounded like an incantation, but they were devoid of strength and intention and would become host to nothing. At most, the man was essentially talking to himself, hidden between two buildings. Might as well let these men continue to hole up in the narrow backstreets, all the while under the illusion that they were enjoying the big, wide world.

Mahito turned away and continued toward home.

"Why did Gregor turn into a bug?"

Mahito didn't look up from his book as he asked the question. He was reading a well-known book by Franz Kafka, the story about a human being who one day transforms into an insect.

"Most people think it's allegorical," said the old man.

"Allegorical?"

"An allegory for how society hated him and treated him like an insect. Like an old man who gets deceived and has his eyes burned out."

"Was that a joke?" Mahito asked.

"No, not really."

The old man didn't burn with emotion, but he would respond if Mahito spoke to him. Conversation with him was like talking to a dictionary. He was knowledgeable, and he had the kind of intelligence capable of breaking down that knowledge for conversation. He knew human culture and the subtleties of the spirit. Mahito had been trying to analyze human souls through novels and movies, so he found conversation with the old man to be helpful.

Human beings were prone to sudden anger, and he couldn't understand why they became sad. What made human beings trust—and betray—each other?

Mahito lived according to a different set of ethical principles, so the old man's explanations helped him understand the difficult concepts. The old man wasn't like other human beings, and Mahito was deeply interested in his life experiences.

"Gregor is an insect, so his family tries to keep him hidden, but he crawls out and dies in the end. Why do you think that is, old man?"

"Because you cannot find peace by avoiding life."

"That's Virginia Woolf, isn't it?"

The old man raised his eyebrows at Mahito's recognition of the quote. "You must read a lot. It makes talking to you easy."

"Don't you want to go back to the human world?"

"If you don't have any attachments to that world, there's no need to run around in it and no need to stand and face it," said the old man.

"Ah, I see."

During the entire brief conversation, Mahito did not once look up from the book.

The old man's soul may have been invisible to the eye, but as usual it burned placidly in the darkness. In the dark tunnel, Mahito used the soul's flickering light to read by.

Outside the tunnel, summer was gradually approaching.

The end came suddenly.

One day, Mahito was wandering around town. He picked up a collection of poems and returned to the tunnel to an unexpected disturbance.

He counted one, two, three flickering souls. One was a shape he knew well, but it was extremely faint, like the flame of a dying candle flickering in the wind. Mahito strolled into the tunnel as usual.

As expected, the old man was there, but he was lying on the ground in an odd position. Two young men were standing on either side of him, looking down.

"Whoa, that sucks. Geezer's gonna die." The thin man with long hair didn't sound particularly upset.

"Told you I could kill a man!" the well-built man with the shaved head responded almost cheerfully.

"Yeah, but that was like...on the spur of the moment."

"Yeah, cuz even though he was all feeble and stuff, he got bossy and told us to get out. He was dissin' us, dude. So I *had* to kick him."

The shaven-headed man had the muscular legs of an athlete. To kill an old man with one kick would be as easy for him as crushing an empty can.

The men weren't the slightest bit interested in the old man's life or soul. They had done this without reason, without hate, without malice. They had just happened to stroll in. Then, on a whim, they had committed a violent act. In a sudden fit, they had beaten an old man.

Perhaps that was one expression of human freedom.

Mahito crouched and studied the old man's face. His burned features were swelling from the blunt trauma. But even at this moment, his expression conveyed tranquility.

"Are you dying?" Mahito questioned the old man in a whisper.

"Yes...I believe so..." the old man rasped. He probably didn't have the strength left to make his vocal cords vibrate. The young men were talking loudly, so they didn't hear him.

Mahito examined the old man's soul. It was slowly approaching the end of its life without hesitation or anger. Mahito was impressed.

The old man was free in the truest sense. He had liberated himself from all the chains of this world, and that hadn't changed even on the threshold of death. Mahito was relieved to confirm that with his own eyes. He observed the old man's dying moments the way one might gaze at a flower wilting.

However...

"Hey, old man?"

Mahito had a premonition.

It was like turning the page of a book to an unexpected development, or realizing what's inside an ornamental box the moment before you open it. Disquiet filled his breast. Instinctive alarm bells warned Mahito to stop watching, and he almost did, but everything continued to race toward the end.

"I...expected to die...alone."

The old man's soul wavered. A smile formed on his swollen features.

"But there's someone here...to watch an old man...give up the ghost."

It was like watching a single drop ripple the surface of water, an inconsequential event. Yet it was the moment of the old man's death. Here at the end of the very end, the old man's soul metabolized.

"Thank...you..."

And then the old man died with a smile on his lips.

Mahito sat motionless for a moment, his eyes wide.

He had thought the old man was different from other human beings. He had thought the old man was truly free. He had thought the old man had reached a special state of release from all worldly bonds, a state of spiritual enlightenment.

But a bond had claimed him at the moment of death.

A solitary death eluded the old man and he had clung to another being as he expired. The old man had turned out to be just another human being. He died satisfied, perhaps as was proper for a human being.

Mahito said nothing. He felt cold inside, as if a wind were blowing through him. He didn't know what word human beings would use to describe this feeling, but his consciousness was like a tangled thread, quivering and then suddenly untangling. All that remained was the feeling of standing in an arid wasteland.

"Anyway," said the man with the shaved head. "The cops won't bother with an old man no one knows anything about."

"Y-y-yeah, I s'pose not!" The long-haired man sounded chipper.

"Besides, the old bastard's the one who started it!"

"Got what he deserved, yeah? Shoulda looked us in the eye when he was talkin' to us!"

"Even worse, he got my pants grimy when I kicked him!" said the man with the shaved head.

"Aw, don't mind that little thing! You crack me up, you killer!"

"He wasn't no *person* tho'. And you know I like to keep clean. Crap... Does blood come out? Water ain't enough."

"I doubt it," said the long-haired man. "But now that the action's over I'm hungry. Let's hit a convenience store."

"Think I could get some good detergent there?"

"Like *I* know! You can look for it after we nab some box lunches."

Mahito stood up suddenly, as if he had finished searching for something on a low shelf. He felt weary to the bone.

The voices echoing in the tunnel were irresponsible, oblivious to reality, incoherent, and drowning out the murmur of the water.

With a languid movement, as if picking up a piece of trash, Mahito approached the shaven-headed man. He used his cursed technique.

Idle Transfiguration.

He struck the man's back. His victim had time to cry out in surprise and pain before he stopped being human.

Simply killing him would leave a corpse that would clutter up the place, so Mahito folded him down to a size that would fit in the palm of his hand. He could throw the man away later. Then, with a broad wave of his hand, he folded up the other man too.

After that, all was quiet.

Mahito picked up the men, who were now the size of chess pieces, and looked down at the old man's body. The old-timer was no more than a meat sack full of bones. The body no longer held a soul for Mahito to alter via Idle Transfiguration.

For a moment, Mahito pondered the not inconsiderable problem of disposing of the body.

The only sound in the tunnel was the water.

The sky looked endless.

Mahito could see the clouds between the buildings. As the wind blew, they drifted along pleasantly.

Mahito was wandering around town again.

"Maybe I should go see a movie. It's been a while."

He chose a small, old-looking theater and snuck inside.

He'd been more motivated recently, as if an unnecessary burden had fallen from his soul, leaving him lighter. And because of that, he'd been tinkering with human beings more often.

He had started thinking that if he could shrink people, then maybe he could enlarge them too, so he'd spent a whole night trying that out. It had been fun, but he thought maybe he'd gotten a little too involved. He wouldn't push himself too hard.

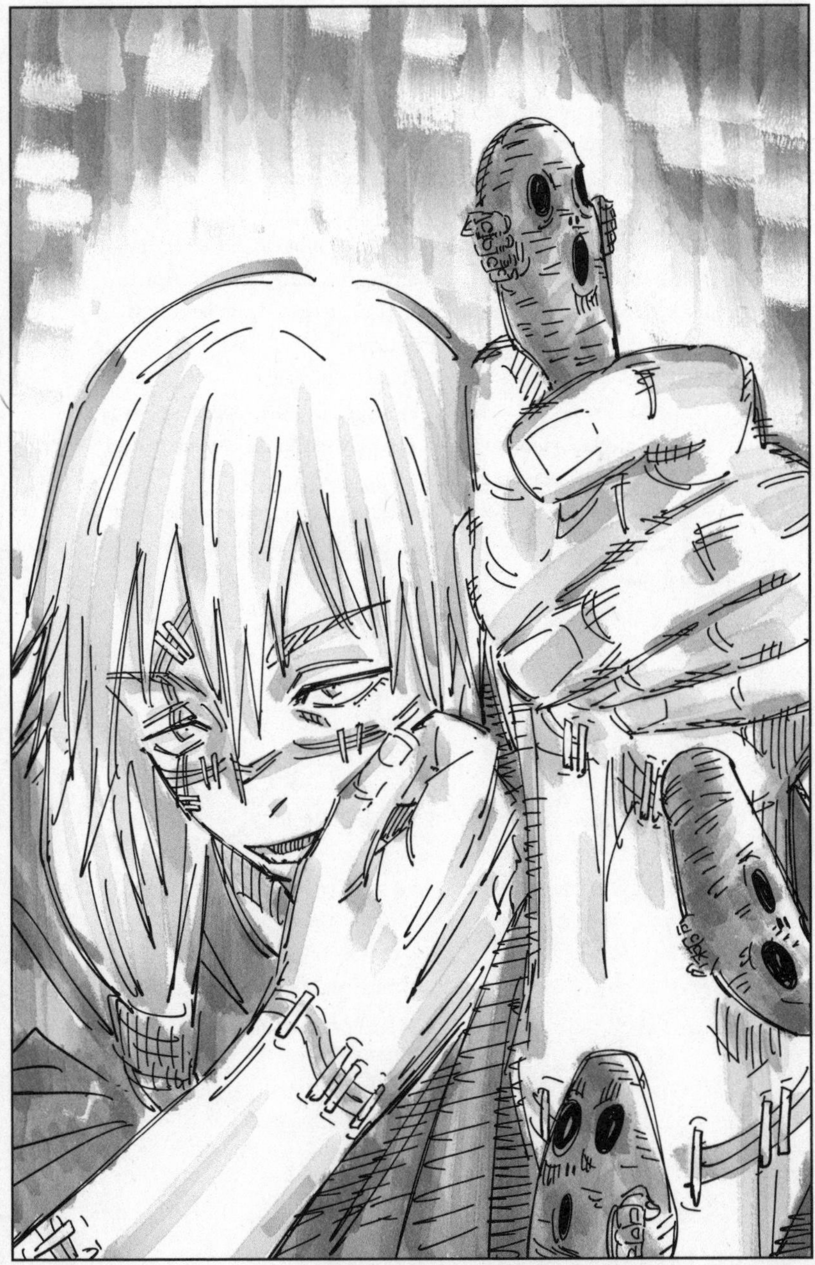

Sometimes you need a change of pace.

He had no idea what movie was showing. It was probably a minor and unimpressive flick, but if he didn't expect too much, he might just find the story surprisingly entertaining. He had a funny feeling he would.

As he walked down the hall, he absentmindedly reached into a pocket and felt the small human figures. They were starting to bulk up. He couldn't have them getting in the way, so he tossed them aside in the movie theater's lobby.

He opened a door and stepped into the theater.

Not many people were in the audience, perhaps because it was a weekday. Some human forms, possibly students, were dispersed throughout the seating area.

Mahito stood in a corner and waited for the images to appear on the screen. Then darkness descended, signaling the start of the film.

CHAPTER 4 Ijichi at Work

CHAPTER 4 Ijichi at Work

The weather was unseasonably hot for the end of August. Itadori was sprawled on the couch.

"*Ugh...*"

The heat wasn't really that bad. In fact, the air-conditioner made it cool. Itadori wasn't in the handy underground theater that Gojo had prepared. He was in an apartment somewhere in the city.

Specifically, he was in Ijichi's room.

I have to go on a little business trip. It isn't close, so I may be gone for a few days. It probably isn't great to hide in the same place indefinitely, so stick by Ijichi's side for a while. You may even have some fun.

That's what Gojo had said. And that's how Itadori ended up crashing at Ijichi's place for a few days. It was his first day, and he was already bored. If it is true that boredom is poison to the human heart, then Itadori had already received a fatal dose.

"Urm..."

Lately Itadori hadn't had enough time to be bored. Since coming to Jujutsu High, he'd sparred with Fushiguro and Kugisaki, exorcized cursed spirits, almost died, and then *actually* died.

After the resurrection, Gojo had made him go into hiding,

which had mostly consisted of watching movies. In fact, it had actually been kind of fun, and had even served as a kind of sorcery training. The last few months had been a roller-coaster ride.

Then, suddenly, he had to start living at Ijichi's, where there was shockingly little to do. Even after Ijichi came home, the man spent most of his time staring at a computer screen.

"Whatcha doin'? Readin' a blog?"

Itadori leaned over Ijichi's shoulder for a look. All he saw was a chart—a jam-packed list of numbers, so detailed it looked like the composite eye of an insect. Petty cash accounting, standard monthly remuneration, depreciable assets, changes to school grounds, cash flow, taxes, faxes, and schmaxes...

Itadori couldn't make any sense of it. Apparently Ijichi was hard at work, which meant Itadori shouldn't make much noise.

"Ijichi, mind if I read a book?" he asked

"Not at all. Take whatever you want from the bookshelves."

"Is this one called *Leviathan* a fantasy novel?"

"No. It's assigned reading in political philosophy," Ijichi said.

"You got any manga?"

"My parents have some old ones back home."

The situation was desperate.

Itadori found a book that looked vaguely like a novel, read a few pages, realized it wasn't for him, and quit. With no other recourse, he flipped on the TV and turned the volume down low. It was that stretch between the daytime variety shows and the prime time shows when there was nothing good on. As he surfed channels, all he saw were news programs and a show in which celebrities sampled tasty cuisine. By process of elimination, he settled on the food show.

"It feels weird to be watching TV at this time of day," he said.

"Yes, you're usually at school."

Itadori was surprised that Ijichi had responded. Maybe a little light conversation wouldn't interfere with Ijichi's work after all.

"And this is when you're usually at work, right?" he said.

"This is within my work hours, yes. But I can work at home as long as it doesn't impact my efficiency. Most companies probably aren't so lax."

"Oh, really?"

Itadori had dealt with adult sorcerers, but as a student, he didn't have much knowledge of more typical office work. Not really getting it, he titled his head and looked back at the television.

"Oh, hey! Takada-chan's the guest!"

"Is she famous?"

Itadori had spoken under his breath, but Ijichi replied anyway. If the man was interested, Itadori thought this might be an effective way to kick off a conversation.

"Yeah, she's been showing more skin lately because she just does whatever she wants. She's cute, but she's tall, so you might not notice it. I love that incongruity."

"Oh, is that what's trendy these days?" asked Itadori.

"Come to think of it, she had a small role in that drama that used to be on at nine o'clock on Monday nights."

"Oh, really?"

"Don't you watch TV dramas, Ijichi?"

"Sorry, but not really. It's not that I dislike them per se, but the new style doesn't appeal to me. I did watch *Pure Vacation* though."

"Hm? When was that on?"

"A little over ten years ago," Ijichi said. "Actually, Motoko-chan was tall too."

"Motoko-chan?"

"She was a popular actress back then, but she got married and gave up her career," Ijichi explained. I suppose kids today wouldn't know her."

"Y-yeah... Are there any variety shows you like?"

"No, not really. I never recognize any of the guests because I don't watch any of the dramas."

"Professional athletes show up too, you know," Itadori said.

"I don't watch sports either. I'm not very athletic, so they just don't interest me."

"If you don't watch prime time, you must watch late-night programming. I like those shows around midnight that showcase new entertainers. I know I'll regret it in the morning, but I stay up late anyway."

"No, I don't watch those either," Ijichi said.

"Then what *do* you watch?"

"The news. But I do like uncool *rakugo* shows."

"Rakugo, huh?"

Itadori had run out of things to say.

Rakugo aired on Sunday evenings when most students were out having fun, so even for a TV child like Itadori, it wasn't an option. Furthermore, the way Ijichi had tacked on rakugo after mentioning the news made it seem like he was going out of his way to be considerate.

Itadori was usually good at getting a conversation started, but he realized their interests were completely different and clammed up. Glancing over, he noticed Ijichi had not stopped typing as they talked. It would be awkward to keep forcing him to speak.

On the TV, the regular presenter and Takada-chan were engaging in banter about the food around Nagoya.

The program was neither entertaining nor boring, so Itadori wouldn't say Takada-chan was at her best. All she ever said about the food was, "Delicious!"

Takada-chan's on, so they should have come up with a better topic. I bet this is all scripted. It's more like a commercial than real reactions to food. But people watch these programs more for the conversation than the food!

Itadori had grown up in front of the boob tube. He had also just binged a ton of movies, so he had developed a sense for quality and was learning to pick up on what the creators were trying to achieve. Which meant boring material was now even more boring.

If this was his only option besides the news, he was in a bad situation. But nothing else was on. Itadori kept watching in hopes that something would catch his interest, but the warm room and soft sofa were making him drowsy.

"Itadori? I have to go out on business."

Itadori started upright. "*Uaaaagh!* Metal Tamori!"

"Metal Tamori?" Ijichi gave him a puzzled look.

"Oops, sorry! I guess I was nodding off. I was having the weirdest dream!"

"What kind of dream was it?!"

"It's kinda fuzzy now," Itadori responded. "Anyway, we're going out?"

"If you're sleepy, there's no need to force yourself. Feel free to stay here and sleep."

"N-no, I wanna go out! I need to photosynthesize!"

"Um, human beings aren't built for that." said Ijichi.

"Oh right...and I can't let anyone know I'm alive."

"Right. But while you shouldn't be walking around in a slapdash disguise, a little drive wouldn't hurt. Gojo did say you should get some fresh air soon."

"Oh, he said that?" Itadori rose from the sofa. He was bored stiff and wanted to go outside if at all possible.

"Here, wear these," commanded Ijichi, holding out a pair of sunglasses.

"Cool! Like *Men in Black*!" Itadori accepted the sunglasses, which were a little big. He held them up to the sunlight. "Are these yours, Ijichi?"

"Yes, they are a personal item."

"Do you dress, like, super flashy when you're not working?"

"No, not at all," replied Ijichi. "But curses are extremely perceptive when it comes to eyes. I do a lot of investigative work, so it's important to conceal where I'm looking."

"Oh, I get it. Gojo hides his eyes too."

"No, that's for a different reason."

"Where do they sell blindfolds like that, anyway?" Itadori asked. "If I wore one, would I look like a pro too?"

"I don't think they sell those anywhere."

Itadori put on the sunglasses. Then he looked back and forth

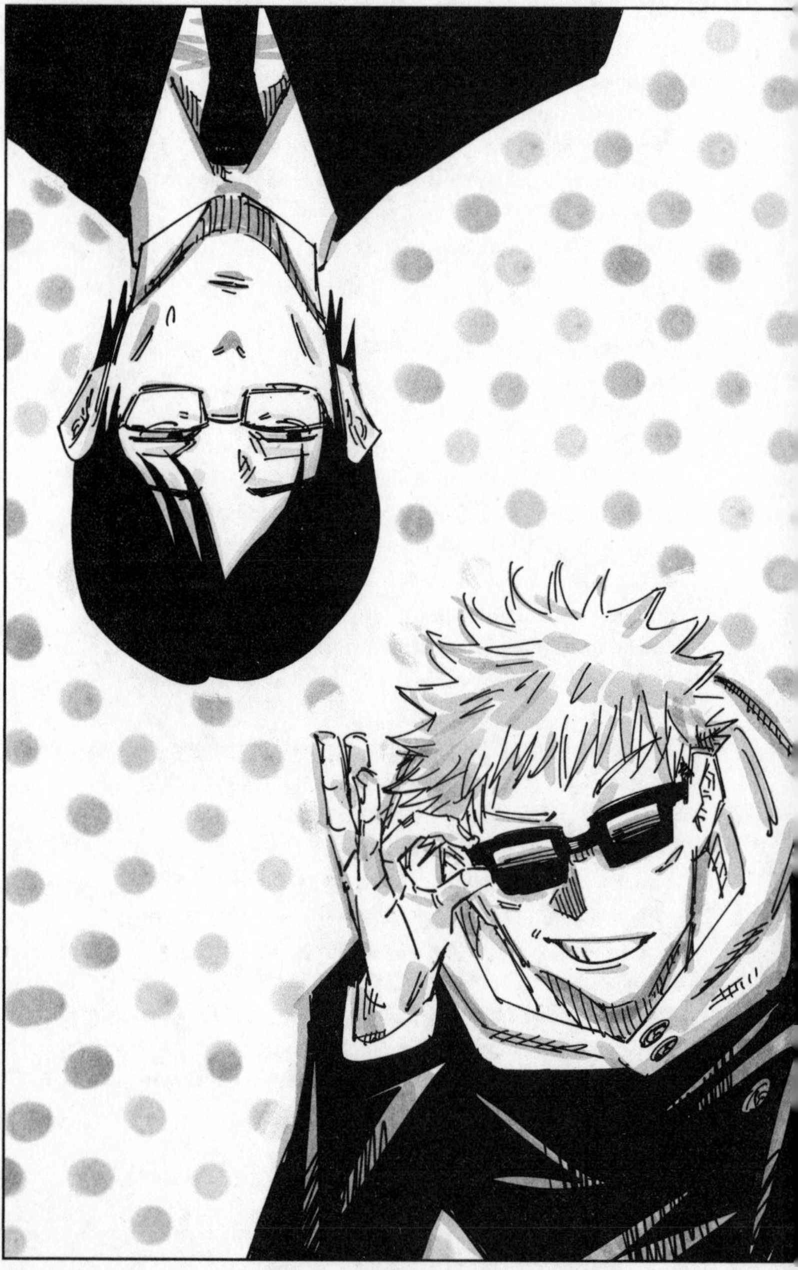

between the mirror and Ijichi. He put a hand to his chin and struck a pose. "How do I look, Ijichi? Like a secret agent?"

"Um…"

Ijichi thought Itadori looked like a young hooligan, but Ijichi was an adult, so he kept this thought to himself.

Itadori hadn't had many opportunities to see Tokyo from the inside of a car. His eyes shone as he gazed at the scenery streaming past the window. Even though he was a TV child, this was more rewarding than a food program about a corner of the country he might never visit.

"Wow. I've never been on the highway in Tokyo."

"The regular streets are kind of crowded at this time of day. Is it really that interesting?" Ijichi asked.

"Yeah! There might be street racers!"

"That doesn't really happen anymore. Where did you hear about that?"

"The game center," Itadori said.

"Ah, of course. Racing games. I used to play those too."

"Oh, is that why you have this expensive car?"

"No, this belongs to Jujutsu High. That's why I'm so careful not to scratch it. I avoid roads where it might get scraped."

"Right," Itadori said, considering this. "Sounds hard."

Itadori sensed that being an adult with a car wasn't as simple as it seemed.

As they engaged in this meandering conversation, which was more than they had managed back at the apartment, Ijichi exited the highway and began threading through streets heavy with traffic. After what Ijichi had said, Itadori worried from his place in the back seat about scratches every time a car came near.

After thirty minutes, they arrived at their destination, a gray building that looked like a stack of boxes.

"Is this the ward office?" Itadori asked.

"Yes. I have to deliver a document."

Ijichi removed a set of documents from his work bag. When Itadori took a look inside the bag, he saw that it was full of even more documents, all meticulously sorted into clear folders and binders.

"That's a lot of docs. Do you really need all those?"

"Yes. The paperwork for submitting to public institutions can be quite hefty."

"Wouldn't it be easier to do online?" asked Itadori.

"Yes, of course. Many things are easier that way. But have you ever noticed how video games each have to be accessed through specific devices and operated in different ways?"

"Yeah, for sure!"

"That's just how electronic data is these days," Ijichi explained, "But paper documents are accessible to everyone in the same format. Besides, even now local government offices tend to place their faith in physical documentation. That's one reason fax machines have never died out."

"Oh, I get it. Hm? Do you have to stamp each one of those? Isn't that a pain in the butt?"

"It does take work, but I can keep copies or get rid of them if I want."

"Right." Itadori wasn't sure whether he understood or not. At the very least, he was beginning to understand that Ijichi was precise and reliable, not one to cut corners. "Anyway, what are those documents?"

"Applications for permission to use sites in need of cursed spirit countermeasures, requests for closure of public facilities, applications for permission to perform roadwork, rosters of on-site personnel with accompanying proof of insurance, and so on."

"Roadwork?" Itadori tilted his head in confusion. It was not a word that Itadori often encountered as a sorcerer and a student.

"Suppose a cursed spirit appears on a mountain road where there's a high incidence of traffic accidents. We need a way to close it," Ijichi explained.

"Can't you just put up a curtain for something like that?"

Itadori thought of the events at the juvenile detention center he had recently visited. A curtain was a barrier used for keeping away ordinary citizens. Itadori vaguely recalled Fushiguro's explanation.

"That would indeed keep people away, but eventually they would begin to wonder why they couldn't use that road."

"Oh, right." Itadori clapped his hands together.

Ijichi pushed up his glasses. "If solving the problem took a long time, people would begin to wonder what was going on. If we don't provide a reason, then something would start to seem out of the ordinary."

"But isn't there, like, a tacit understanding for that kind of thing? I thought Jujutsu High and the metropolitan government would cooperate with each other."

"Yes, but to all appearances, Jujutsu High is a private school, so it requires the documentation of a private school. And if that isn't enough, further documentation is necessary to prove to regular society that nothing unusual is going on. Thus, putting up a sign reading 'Falling Rock Removal' requires paperwork."

"Oh. It's more of a hassle than I thought."

"Of course," Ijichi said. "And I also have to provide explanations in person."

Itadori suddenly realized something: knowledge of the existence of cursed spirits was a normal thing for him now, but Ijichi's comments were reminding him that not long ago, before embarking on the life of a sorcerer, he hadn't known about any of that stuff.

Itadori continued to mull this over as he watched Ijichi get out of the car. Sorcerers fought and exorcized cursed spirits. They did it to protect not just people's lives but their ways of life. Since human fear gave birth to curses, allowing anxiety surrounding the existence of curses to spread would be incredibly dangerous. The human heart was what gave birth to curses. Therefore, preventing fear was important for protecting people.

Itadori may not have put it in such precise terms, but he now saw the situation in a new light, however dim.

It's more difficult than I thought to preserve our regular daily life.

When Ijichi returned from the ward office, Itadori welcomed him with a more erect posture.

"Thank you for waiting, Itadori."

"Uh, welcome back."

Next, Ijichi visited a small building bearing the logo of a soft drink that Itadori recognized.

"Is this a soda company or something?" he asked.

"It's a subcontractor for a business group. They install and supply vending machines."

"Uh...so what're we doing here? Have curses been haunting vending machines?"

"No, but we were passing by, so I thought I would pop in to show my face. This company installs and manages all the vending machines at Jujutsu High," Ijichi said.

"Oh...okay."

At school, Itadori had seen a worker coming and going sometimes. He had never given it much thought, but now he realized that no matter how you looked at that guy, he definitely wasn't directly involved in jujutsu.

"And you have to go to all the trouble of stopping by?"

"Yes, because Jujutsu High is nominally a religious institution. We can't let too many people know about what goes on inside, so once we establish a business relationship like this one, we don't change it. Personal visits to companies you're friendly with are important, Itadori."

"Got it."

"Oh, right!" Ijichi said, suddenly. "Is there a particular drink you like?"

"Me? Um, I like sports drinks. Nothing too sweet," Itadori said.

"Understood. I'll mention that. We don't have many students, so it helps them know what's in demand. Maybe your favorites will be in stock next time you're at school."

"Seriously? Awesome, thanks!"

Itadori bowed as he watched Ijichi walk into the office building.

When Ijichi returned a few minutes later, a good-natured man in work clothes was with him. Apparently, he had wanted to see Ijichi off. Itadori watched the man offer a polite bow, which Ijichi returned. For a moment, Itadori thought maybe he should join in. Then he remembered he was officially dead at the moment.

A moment later, Ijichi climbed back in the car. "Thanks for waiting, Itadori. Let's go."

"Yeah, okay."

As Ijichi drove away, Itadori looked out from the back seat through the darkened glass. The man in work clothes was politely bowing toward the car. He was probably in management now, but his hands looked like they had done manual labor.

Itadori recalled visiting the ward office earlier.

Normal people had no connection to cursed spirits. The employees of that company, however, visited Jujutsu High, which meant they lived at the edge of an *abnormal* life.

Itadori felt a tightening in his chest at the thought. The man visible through the window was much smaller now. From inside the car, Itadori bowed his head to him.

Ijichi suddenly stopped the car at the side of the road.

"What's up, Ijichi?"

"Um, excuse me."

Ijichi pulled a vibrating phone from his pocket, and Itadori realized someone was calling him. He wondered who it could—

"Hello? This is he. Good work, Gojo. What do you need?"

Ijichi at Work

"Gojo Sensei?" Itadori wondered.

Gojo was on a business trip somewhere far away, but Itadori didn't know much about where or why he had gone. He tried to listen in on the call.

"A detour? Why? Oh, I see. Hold on a second. I'll look it up and call you back."

Ijichi ended the call. He pulled a memo pad from his breast pocket and looked at it while scrolling through the contacts on his phone.

"Ijichi, what's up with Gojo?" Itadori asked.

"He went to see someone, but changed course along the way, so he needs me to look up the window in that area."

"Window? I feel like I should know what that is, but..."

"A window is someone who isn't a sorcerer, but who is related to Jujutsu High and who can see curses. Windows can trace curses and assist investigations."

"Oh, okay," said Itadori. "I heard about that when we went to the detention center."

Ijichi's shoulders tensed, and his fingers, which had been flipping memo pages, froze.

"What's wrong Ijichi?"

"Oh...never mind. It's nothing."

"Hey, why do you have both a memo pad *and* a smartphone?"

"Well, the smartphone is in alphabetical order, but I need to know who's in which area, and that's difficult. For that, I use the addresses in the memo pad," Ijichi said.

"Which area? We're not only talking about Tokyo? Don't tell me you have to know about all the windows all over Japan!"

"Usually, I wouldn't have to, but Gojo is always asking me about them, so..." Ijichi trailed off.

"Oh...now I understand."

"You know, that guy has a good memory and he's intelligent, but he refuses to make the effort to remember anything. That includes window addresses for sure, but he even asks me about sweets at convenience stores and train timetables."

"Sounds awful. Seriously."

Itadori could easily imagine Gojo making ridiculous requests.

While they were talking, Ijichi must have found the information he was looking for, because he called Gojo back.

"Um...hello? Gojo? In that area—Hey, I did it as fast as I could! Yes, I did once call you back in under a minute, but—What do I care if your ice cream melted while you were waiting?! Why would you *slap* me when you get back?! Make a memo for it?! How can you say that to me?! No, I refuse to schedule myself for a completely unjustified lecture! So just forget it!"

"Whoa..."

Within the confines of the car, Itadori could clearly overhear Gojo chewing out Ijichi. The ridiculousness of it even got on Itadori's nerves.

"Huh? Yes. Now that you mention it, you used the principal's cursed corpse for Itadori's training. What about it? Huh? You took that without permission?! And you want me to put it back?! Where is—It's lying out in the open in the basement?! Huh? Well, first... Yes...uh-huh...mm-hmm...understood. I'll be sure to fetch it. Hm? You added more movies to the film collection? No, you can't claim that as a business expense! No. Absolutely not. Out of the question. Yes, uh-huh, yes, I'll do my best."

Today, Ijichi was running errands both large and small. Itadori stared at him intently.

That guy sure has it rough.

As they were hustling around Tokyo, the sun outside the car windows was sinking deeper and deeper. When it finally went behind the buildings, the light from the streetlights became brighter.

"Man, we've been all over today!" Itadori said.

"Yes, it took longer than I expected. I'd hoped things would go a little more smoothly."

"Well, that's Gojo Sensei's fault!"

"Yes, I suppose it is," Ijichi said.

"He *is* dependable, but he's not much of an adult."

"You're not wrong about his dependability. He's strong and kind, but he has a way of, you know, pushing people to the limit."

"Yeah, I totally get that!"

"Yet he also has a soft spot for you students," Ijichi noted.

"Definitely," Itadori agreed. "He's always done all right by me."

"Agreed. I hate to admit it, but he's talented and charismatic. Many of the sorcerers look up to him. Although I do hate to admit it."

"You said that twice."

The relationship between Itadori and Ijichi had warmed since their time stuck in the apartment together. Maybe it had something to do with the experience of being out for a drive. The loose atmosphere made it easier to talk, so Itadori said what was on his mind.

"You sure have a busy schedule, Ijichi."

Ijichi responded with a half-smile. "Did I look that busy to you?"

"Well, you calculate stuff and handle documents and visit people and serve as Gojo Sensei's errand boy and—"

"That bit about 'errand boy' was unnecessary."

"Sorry," Itadori said. "But despite being so busy, you don't do much sorcerer-type work."

"Ha ha! It's pretty unexciting, isn't it?"

"Honestly, yes!"

"I admire your bluntness," Ijichi said. "Anyway, fighting is outside my expertise."

"And Gojo Sensei makes up for it by pushing all sorts of work onto you."

"Yes, I guess he does."

Itadori could see Ijichi's eyes in the rearview mirror, and for a moment they looked cold. Worried that he might have said the wrong thing, Itadori looked away.

"It isn't so bad," Ijichi said. "If I were doing more work typical of a sorcerer... The thing is, sorcerers and Jujutsu High staff tend to think of themselves as detached from society."

"Yeah, I sorta realized that today," Itadori said.

"But we *are* part of society, which means attending to countless details and dull chores."

"Yeah, I can see that now." Itadori nodded as he gazed at the streetlights passing by.

As the night deepened, the number of lights increased.

With its hundreds of thousands of lights, the city looked like the night sky descended to Earth. Each light signified human activity. They spread from this city throughout Japan and across the world. Jujutsu High was a place that faced the darkness, but it existed amidst the lights of all these people. Itadori truly understood that now.

"Thank you, Ijichi," he said.

"What made you say that all of a sudden?"

"Your work really is unexciting."

"Yes, what about it? Did that need repeating?" Ijichi said.

"It's just, I realized that thanks to your unexciting, painstaking work, sorcerers retain ties to the rest of the world. I'm thankful for that."

"You are, huh?" Ijichi's voice was faint. The lights of passing cars reflected in his glasses, making it hard to see his eyes, but his face in the rearview mirror didn't have a bright expression.

For a time, the only sounds in the car came from the vehicle's tires racing across the asphalt and the music from the radio on the car stereo. The chorus to the current song was one Itadori had heard countless times. After the lyrics ended, the catchy pop melody continued for a while before eventually fading away. When that happened, it felt like the mood in the car had also somehow changed.

Now it was Ijichi who initiated a conversation. "Um, Itadori? You shouldn't thank me. Instead, I should apologize."

"Huh? What for?" He had never imagined an apology was necessary and couldn't guess the reason. The childlike, ingenuous expression on his face showed his utter confusion.

Ijichi frowned. His next words came haltingly. "The other day, I sent you into a deadly situation."

"Oh, that?"

Itadori recalled the series of fights against the special grade cursed spirit. That had indeed been a bitter experience, but he didn't hold it against Ijichi.

Ijichi's voice only became more grave. "I said it was merely an evacuation. I also warned you not to engage. I didn't mean to fail in my obligations as assistant manager. But at the very least, that was no place to send first-years. And you were the resulting sacrifice."

"Yeah, but...I'm right here, alive and well, aren't I?"

"After having died once." Ijichi's voice trembled.

Itadori had wanted to laugh this off, but when he heard that tremble, he shut up. He had lost people close to him, and he himself had died. As yet, however, Itadori had never experienced someone else dying through *his* fault. Nonetheless, a feeling of heart-wrenching regret washed over him.

"I told you it wouldn't be so bad, but I'm a sorcerer who can't fight—an adult whose job is sending students, all younger than I am, on dangerous missions. You may have come back from the dead, but I will send you back into battle." The sound of the engine drowned out the sound of Ijichi swallowing. "As an adult, I want to lend seamless support to your missions, and I'll try to do better."

"Ijichi..."

Maybe this was an apology, or maybe it was a justification. But what Itadori had seen of Ijichi's work today was a form of atonement and proof of the man's dedication.

"I vow to do my job," Ijichi said.

Ijichi's unsteady voice was deeply apologetic and low, as if a weight were crushing it. It didn't have Gojo's dependability or the principal's severity. Instead, it expressed intense worry and sincerity.

Ijichi couldn't fight, but he would never allow himself to say, *I won't let you die again.* Despite how he felt, he had to send Itadori on more missions.

Itadori had no idea how disheartening that must've been to a conscientious adult. He did understand, however, that Ijichi's words expressed his innermost feelings and carried the meaning of what he most wanted to convey. So he received them, accepted them, and smiled.

"Like I said. Thanks, Ijichi." Itadori spoke softly as he looked at his reflection in the window. "I'll probably keep being reckless and make you worry, but that's my choice. I'm not gonna stop."

"That's just how you are, right?"

"Yeah, but I'm gonna get stronger so you don't have to worry about me forever, Ijichi. And you'll help me, won't you? With the things I don't understand or know? And stuff that takes more than fighting to solve?"

"Yes, I will," Ijichi said.

His hands trembled on the wheel. Itadori pretended not to notice. He figured adults didn't want children to see such things.

Instead, Itadori kept talking in a bright voice. "Are you going home now, Ijichi?"

"Yes. I'm getting hungry though, and since you're already in disguise, we should probably eat out."

"Are you sure that's okay?" Itadori asked.

"Well, we're already out, aren't we? Besides, it must have been boring for you to just have to watch me today."

"Ha ha! Sounds good! You know me well."

Ijichi at Work

"Itadori, what would you like to eat?"

"Meat!"

"That's a sensible answer," replied Ijichi. "Steak or *yakiniku*, which will it be?"

"That's the ultimate dilemma. Wait twenty minutes while I think about it."

"That's too long."

Their laughter filled the vehicle.

The car's tail lights streamed through the night as if shaking off teardrops.

CHAPTER 5 Illusory Trek to the Guardian Demon

The night air was cold and still, as if time had frozen.

The lingering scent of summer was growing more distant with each passing day, and the slight breeze across the asphalt was dry. Under the streetlights, Itadori was out for a walk, listening to the distant noise of the city, alone and without any particular destination.

Gojo said he intended to reveal Itadori's survival soon, so he didn't mind if Itadori went for walks when there weren't many people around. Itadori had "died" once, but after his long period in hiding, simply taking a walk for no specific purpose felt luxurious.

It was nine o'clock at night, and the moon was high.

Itadori avoided the area around Jujutsu High and the city center, where school personnel might see him, choosing instead to walk around a quiet bedroom village. The busy areas of the city would be at their liveliest at this time, but in this residential area, there were few pedestrians or cars. All human activity felt closed away. Occasionally, he heard voices coming from inside the houses, and this was pleasing to his ears.

He'd walked quite a long way, and was thinking it was time to head back. Itadori turned when he reached a large road and started up a lane that was one road over from the one by which he had come.

Even this slight change of route came with a change of scenery. Looking up at the power lines, he wondered vaguely where all the crows went each night. He walked and walked without aim. The colors of the houses slowly passed in the corners of his vision.

After about ten minutes, he came to an open space.

"Oh, there's a park here?"

The park Itadori had discovered seemed to have been squeezed in between the surrounding residences. There was a slide and a jungle gym and an unnaturally empty space where a merry-go-round might have once stood. To Itadori, the park's offerings looked meager.

From nearby, he heard the squeak of metal against metal. He turned and saw a single swing moving, and not because of the wind. A small form sat there, swinging back and forth in the glow of an old streetlight.

He looks too mature for an elementary school student. Maybe he's in junior high?

As the boy swung, his naturally wavy hair, trimmed short, flipped back and forth.

Itadori could tell from the gentle rhythm of his swinging and the expression on the boy's face that he wasn't swinging for fun.

Itadori stared at the boy for the space of a few blinks, then walked toward him. "Hey, what's up?"

"Huh?"

The boy looked up.

At first glance, he appeared to be wary. Itadori wore a uniform over his hoodie and had bleached his hair. The boy may have thought he had attracted the attention of a delinquent. However, when Itadori reached the streetlight, it revealed his face and his innate friendliness, and the boy's facial expression softened.

"Were you thinking about something?" Itadori asked.

"Uh, yeah. I guess so."

Itadori sat beside the boy on the swing set. It creaked under his weight, which was more than usual for the swing. The playground equipment was for children, so it was a little snug for a big high school student.

"Seems like you're nervous talking to someone whose face and name you don't know. I'm Yuji Itadori."

"I'm Kairi Minato."

"Cool name."

"My grandma who died last year said that people romanticize the ocean, so I'm named after it," the boy explained.

"Your grandmother was a romantic, huh? It's a good name."

"Yes, she was a unique person," the boy said. "She said she once clashed with a bear. And she *won*."

"She must have had a strong personality."

Itadori's expression changed as the conversation about the boy's life proved to be more interesting than he had expected. The thought occurred to him that death comes even to strong grandparents who act cool. But he hadn't forgotten why he came over.

"Well, your grandmother may have been cool, but your mom and dad may be stricter. It's pretty late. Aren't they worried about you?"

"Oh..."

Kairi might have been expecting such a comment. Looking up at the streetlight, he made a face as if to say, *Okay, here we go...*

The light flickered. Perhaps the filament was old. The way it lit the bugs around it, which seemed like relics that summer had left behind, reminded Itadori of an old movie.

Itadori continued swinging as he waited for the boy's answer. He pushed off the ground with his feet, and the swing moved back and forth with a creaking sound. It felt comfortable, like a cradle; it might indeed be a good place for thinking.

After the space of a few breaths, Kairi spoke. "I can't go back home."

"Did you fight with your parents?" Itadori asked.

"No. I mean *physically*."

"Physically? Is it too far or something?"

"No, it's nearby," Kairi said. "Will you promise not to laugh if I tell you?"

"I won't laugh. After all, *you* aren't laughing about it."

Kairi relaxed his uneasy frown at the tone of Itadori's voice. Rather than being critical, Itadori had sounded as if it was only natural to believe the boy.

Nonetheless, it seemed that what Kairi was about to say was no laughing matter.

After a stretch of silence, Kairi took a deep breath and finally stated the problem. "There's a demon there."

"A demon?"

"It appears in front of the house at night. It's only...about this big though." Kairi cupped the air as though he were holding a beach ball.

The scale was so precise that Itadori could tell the boy had a real object in mind, as if he really saw the form of a demon in the darkness.

Kairi frowned apologetically. "Totally unbelievable, right?

"No, I believe you."

"Huh?"

"If you say a demon's there, it's there," Itadori asserted. "I can tell by looking at you that it's really bothering you. Sort of, anyway."

"You believe me?"

Itadori searched his memory. He didn't think he had a great deal of life experience, but he had encountered a lot of curses. Strong curses and weak curses in a staggering variety. By contrast, this appeared to be an ordinary residential area, and judging from Kairi's description, the "demon" wasn't that big. Given these factors, he thought Kairi's curse probably wasn't very powerful. Considering that Kairi had seen it without suffering any damage, it might be a fly head, grade 3 at most.

"Well, I've seen similar things myself. A *lot*." Itadori gave a strong kick and swung two, three times for momentum, then jumped off. "So shall we go?"

"Huh? Go? Where to?"

"Your house."

"But there's a demon there!" Kairi explained.

"Don't worry. I'll go with you. If it looks really bad, we'll turn back. But we can get close enough for a look, right?"

Itadori didn't have anything particularly difficult in mind. The expectation of a victory, of appearing cool, or even fulfilling his duty as a sorcerer were the furthest things from his mind. He had only one simple thought.

"It sucks when you can't go home," he said.

Itadori decided to help someone else because of that simple belief.

He and Kairi walked for about ten minutes.

As they advanced through the night breeze, they engaged in chitchat for distraction, speaking about everything from clubs at school to their favorite movies and manga.

Illumination from streetlights dotted the darkness enveloping the neighborhood. One streetlight shone directly in front of the gate to a house. It was a simple house, deep blue with a triangular roof.

As soon as it came into view, Kairi stopped walking.

"There it is."

He spoke with a struggle, through a dry throat. Instinctive tension froze his legs in place.

Itadori walked up behind him, then stepped forward and turned his eyes toward the entrance to the house, illuminated amidst the darkness.

A dark form sluggishly stepped from the shadow of the gate-posts. Smaller than a human being, it lacked the charm of a small animal. It seemed unnatural, with a twisted external appearance that caused revulsion to well up from within Itadori's soul.

Without a doubt, it was a curse.

"Moooooom!" it cried out.

It had two mouths where its eyes should be. Its nose looked to have been shaved off. It didn't have any ears, and its main mouth was sutured shut with stitches. Its body was composed of exposed muscle tissue, short legs, a small trunk, and long, thick arms that ended in massive fists.

Two distorted projections that looked like bundles of blood vessels extended from its temples like horns.

No wonder Kairi thought it was a demon.

The two distorted mouths gnashed their teeth, and the demon roared threateningly.

"Tryyyyyy agaaaaaaaaaaaaaaaaaaain."

"Um...Itadori?" Kairi's voice was shaking with fear.

Itadori stepped between the demon and Kairi as if to block the boy and loosely spread his arms wide as if to soothe the demon. "Don't worry. I got this."

This cursed spirit, this "demon," wasn't a strong curse. A precise evaluation would probably rate it grade 3. He couldn't just overlook it, but it wasn't something he couldn't handle, either.

He decided he would exorcize it in the most uneventful way possible.

It wasn't that he wanted to show off how easy it was or that he took this lightly. He just wanted to put Kairi at ease. He wanted to wipe away the boy's fear, calm his nerves, and send him home. That was all Itadori had in mind.

"Stay back, Kairi."

When Itadori's hands formed fists, the demon also warmed up for action. It flexed its short legs and swung its arms in broad arcs, up and down. Then it did something like a squat and sprung up, jumping high, high into the air. Its unusual silhouette blocked the moonlight.

"Tryyyyyy agaaaaaaaaaaaaaaaaaaain."

Using the momentum from its fall, the demon struck downward with both hands as if they were hammers. The attack was so simple that Itadori dodged with a casual sidestep.

The demon's body may have been small, but its long arms were a threat. It swung them to the side. Without breaking a sweat, Itadori stepped back, putting distance between them.

"Tryyyyyy agaaaaaaaaaaaaaaaaaaain."

As if already tiring of this, the demon threw a straight punch.

"Enough already!" Itadori shouted.

Seeing that simple attack as an opportunity, Itadori twisted and swung. He dodged the demon's fists, closed the distance, and drove his fist into its torso.

Divergent Fist!

The demon's small form lifted in the air.

"Mooooooooooooooooooooooo—*agh!*"

The second impact, charged with cursed energy, struck it a moment later. The demon flew up and burst apart as if struck by an invisible cannonball. The battle in the residential neighborhood had ended so quickly that it was a bit of a letdown.

"Heh!" Itadori chortled. "All finished!"

"Huh? Um, what just happened?!" Kairi asked.

"I wasted its ass. So you can go home now."

For a moment, Kairi blinked his eyes at Itadori, who was grinning.

Kairi seemed hesitant, but after a few seconds of silence in the night, he bowed deeply. "Thank you." His voice suggested that he was still confused, but he expressed his thanks anyway. Bowing over and over, he went into the house.

Itadori smiled and watched him go. His nighttime stroll had grown a little long, but now he could finally head home. As they parted, however, Itadori couldn't help but wonder why the look on Kairi's face was the same one he'd worn earlier when he was alone in the park.

A few days later, Itadori was walking around town again. A simple walk wasn't that interesting, but he did enjoy the time alone. He changed the route every time he went out, and today found himself revisiting that neighborhood.

Oh, right... I had a minor dustup here the other night.

Perhaps because he had been recalling the incident, his steps had naturally set him walking down the same streets. Just like before, he turned the corner. Just like before, he walked the same path. Just like before, he arrived at the same park.

And he couldn't believe his eyes.

"Kairi?"

The boy was sitting on a swing and hanging his head.

Kairi was sitting in the park, staring at the streetlight, and wearing the same glum expression.

"Oh...Itadori."

"What's wrong? The demon's gone now."

Kairi was speechless as he looked at Itadori apologetically. That was enough for Itadori to sense his unease.

"Surely not!"

Itadori ran out of the park with a sudden burst of speed.

This time, he left Kairi behind and raced down the streets of the neighborhood alone. He swung his arms in great arcs as he rushed through the darkness and tromped across the asphalt. The chilly night air dug into his lungs, making his chest hurt. His heart was pounding, but not from the exertion. Intense internal disquiet was sounding an alarm and driving his footfalls. He ran and ran as hard as he could.

He arrived in front of the house.

"No way!"

Just like the other day, the demon was there. It was the same curse in the same form.

Itadori's suspicion that there had been two curses soon disappeared. He didn't believe this was a different curse with the same external appearance. Its form and presence weren't the least bit different.

"Moooooooooooom!"

Sensing Itadori's eyes on it, the demon leapt high into the sky almost as if reenacting their earlier encounter.

"Why, you...!"

Reflexively evading, Itadori immediately counterattacked and hit the demon with Divergent Fist.

"Mooooooooooooooooom!"

Itadori's body remembered the timing and the opening he could exploit in the demon's attack. His strike was dead-on, and the impact of his cursed energy sent the demon flying.

It was disturbing how easily he had exorcized this demon for a second time.

Itadori opened and closed his fists as he stood and stared. His attack had definitely worked. He had definitely finished it off. He had definitely exorcized it. However, he sensed the exact same presence that he had confronted the other night. He'd been certain he had expelled it then too, certain he had killed it.

If so, then what was the demon I just fought?

"Don't feel too bad about it, Itadori."

Itadori spun around at the sound of the voice. He didn't need a mirror to know how confused he must have looked.

"Kairi?"

"I doubt there's anything you can do."

In contrast to Itadori's voice, which was in the grip of confusion, Kairi's tone was calm. It was laden with resignation and an exhaustion that seemed unfitting for his age.

"I can tell you're really strong, Itadori. But that demon will probably come back again and again. I can't be sure, but I think so."

"What do you mean?"

Kairi looked up at the roof of the house. Itadori followed his line of sight and stared at the roof, and his eyes widened.

"I think the demon is guarding the house. It'll show up here over and over to drive away bad people."

Itadori listened to Kairi's words, but he couldn't comprehend them. He became bewildered and his eyes widened. They saw something he couldn't explain. A familiar silhouette was perched atop the roof as if holding up the moon.

The demon had reappeared yet again.

"Anyway, that's what happened."

"Yeah, okay."

The next day, Itadori told Gojo about the demon.

Itadori had revealed he was still alive to his peers before the Kyoto Sister School Goodwill Event, and now he was leading a relaxed and secluded life in a room that Gojo had arranged for him.

Gojo was in sunglasses and sweats, comfortable clothes for lounging at home, and flipping through the pages of a regional tourism magazine as he listened to what Itadori said.

"Then what?" Gojo asked.

"There's no 'then what,'" Itadori said. "Obviously, a demon that resurrects is beyond my ability. Shouldn't you come with me?"

"Well, I'm busy."

"You don't *look* busy."

Gojo was rolling around the sofa, holding the magazine in both hands, kicking his legs, and somehow also eating *daifuku*.

"Then I'll ask Nanamin," Itadori sighed.

"Don't treat grade 1 sorcerers like your support center."

"Huh?!"

"That demon's a cinch to waste, right? It doesn't sound like this particular cursed spirit has a cursed energy over grade 3. There's no need for me to get involved." said Gojo.

"But it comes back no matter how many times I exorcize it! There haven't been any casualties yet, but if we let it go, something bad might happen, and then it'll be too late!"

"So exorcize it until it doesn't come back anymore."

"If I could do *that*, there'd be no problem!"

"Yuji." Gojo raised his face from the magazine and looked at Itadori from behind his sunglasses. He wasn't wearing his usual flippant smile. "What do you think is the main reason people can't help other people?"

For a moment, Itadori froze. His head filled with memories, as if they were erupting from the pit of his stomach. Countless scenes passed through his mind, so many as to make his visual field flicker.

Warped human beings. Twisted human beings. A mother and son he couldn't save.

He hadn't been able to do anything.

"Because they're weak."

Gojo let out a faint sigh and stood up from the sofa. "That's partially true. But strength and weakness aren't everything."

Gojo only knew about the movie theater and the incident at Satozakura High School from reports he'd heard. However, given the tragic events that had occurred and the harsh reality Itadori had confronted, Gojo could imagine that the boy was bearing a painful burden. Despite his grounding as a sorcerer in body and mind, and despite his unusual physical constitution, Itadori was a teenager who hadn't been in the jujutsu world for long. Training could improve his cursed energy and physical strength, but a heart wasn't so easy to fix. And Gojo didn't want him to stay broken for long.

He approached Itadori, who was hanging his head. "In this world, tragedies too often end in misery, even when it's possible to help. But the problem isn't lack of strength or getting there too late." As Gojo passed Itadori, he patted him on the head without making eye contact. "The main reason it happens is that people forget they have the strength to help."

At those words, Itadori gasped and looked up.

Itadori couldn't say he now understood what the resolution was. Nonetheless, Gojo's words enabled him to take another look at the situation.

Observing this change in Itadori, Gojo smiled with satisfaction. "While we're at it, let's review one more thing. What is the number one thing that gives rise to curses?"

"Um...negative human emotion?"

"If that's true," Gojo responded, "then you already know the answer—namely, that fighting and exorcizing aren't everything."

"Oh. Right."

"One thing I like about you is you're straightforward, so you get to the answers fast."

Gojo's smile was the final push Itadori needed. Now that Itadori's head was clear, his body also felt unobstructed; he was already on the move.

"I'll see ya later, Sensei!"

No sooner had Itadori said farewell than he was racing out into the bright streets.

Gojo watched Itadori depart, then plopped back down on the sofa. He had forgotten what page he was reading.

"It's easy to lend a hand to a child who has fallen, but it's a teacher's job to show a child how to stand up unassisted. It isn't always easy."

Itadori's sincerity was a more significant attribute than his being Sukuna's vessel. As a result, trauma had the potential to become a curse more fearsome than anything else, a nasty curse preventable only by confronting one's own heart. Instead of cradling that heart, Gojo could teach it to be prepared. *That's* what it meant to raise students.

"It's much harder than teaching jujutsu."

Smiling despite his serious thoughts, Gojo downed the rest of his daifuku.

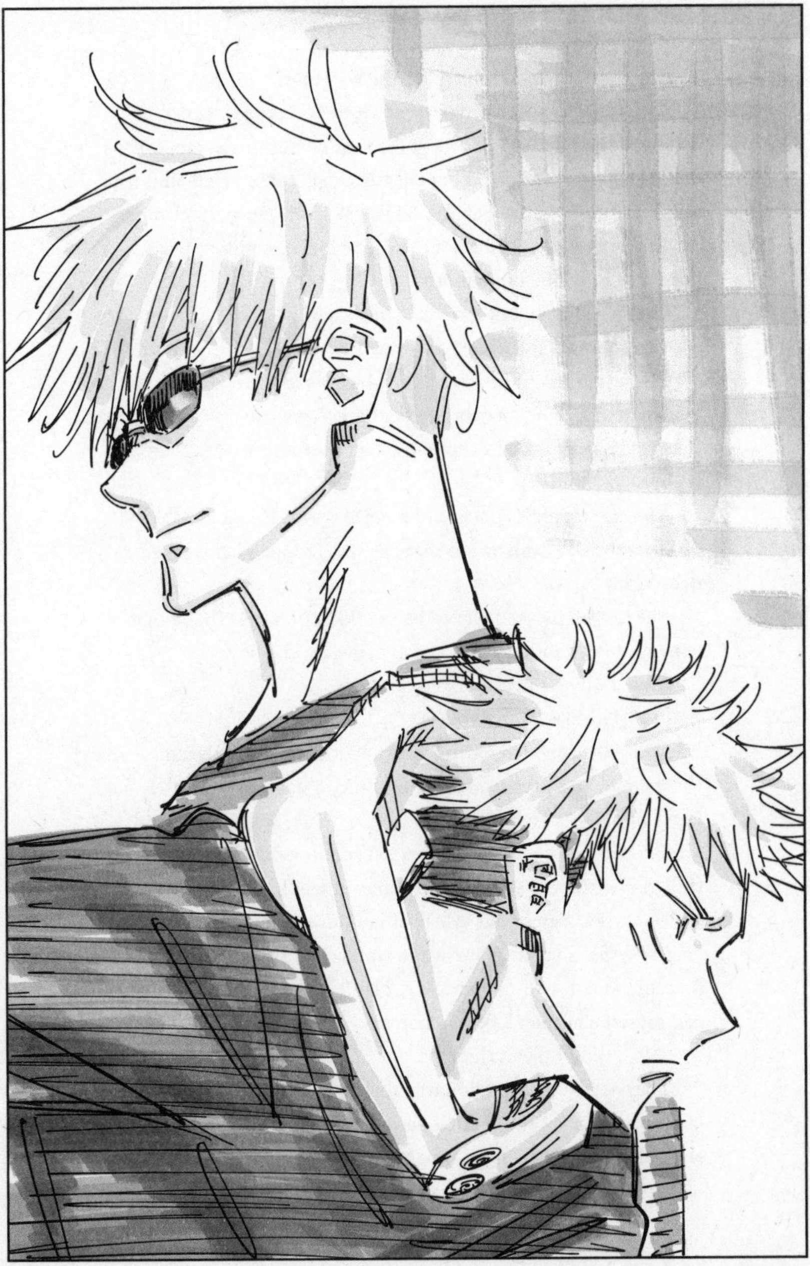

By now, Itadori could remember the way there.

The sun was still up, so the atmosphere in the streets felt different than before. A modest amount of traffic was out, and he could see a few people taking out the trash, taking shopping trips, and standing around chatting. This was likely the perfect time.

In front of Kairi Minato's house, he found someone who appeared to be the boy's mother.

"Are you a friend of Kairi's?" she asked.

"Yes, sort of. Even though we're different ages."

She might have been over forty, but she looked younger at first glance. Itadori could sense her kindness from the way she had asked if he was Kairi's friend despite the fact that Itadori was clearly a high school student.

The curse didn't appear to be bothering the woman. She probably wasn't even aware that she was living in a house where a demon appeared.

She looked pleased just to be speaking of Kairi. That alone conveyed her gentle nature and her love for the boy.

That's why it hurt Itadori to ask this.

"Kairi hasn't come home yet?"

"No." She frowned sadly, but her attitude remained calm. Perhaps the woman was prepared for that topic of conversation. "He *does* come home. It's embarrassing to admit this, but my husband and I don't know *when*. After we started turning the lights off early, though, he started sneaking in sometime before ten o'clock."

"Isn't that dangerous? He's still in junior high, right?"

"Yes, that's right. There was a time when I thought I should go find him and drag him home, but... Isn't it awful? I have no right to call myself a mother," the woman said forlornly.

"No, I didn't mean that."

The woman's expression was so sad it hurt Itadori to see it.

It wasn't responsible for a parent to allow a child to walk around at night. She must have blamed herself for his absence. Itadori could see the sorrow and fatigue in her eyes.

I'm not here to criticize her.

Itadori reevaluated his position and purpose.

"Um, may I ask something unusual? Do you know anything about a demon?"

"A demon?" For a moment, the woman's eyes registered surprise, but they weren't as confused as Itadori had expected. On the contrary, she embraced the topic with surprising ease. "Did you hear about that from Kairi?"

"Yes."

"The demon is a kind of fairy tale his grandmother told him. Or rather, a kind of warning fable. She said a demon would show up where bad children are. I suppose it's like a *namahage* demon."

"Oh, the cool grandmother!" Itadori said, remembering.

"Right, right. I should have known he would tell you about her." The woman laughed with a smile both amused and desolate. Something about her sad expression caught Itadori's attention.

"Kairi must've really loved his grandmother."

"Yes, he did. From his point of view, she was like a replacement for his mother. He's been struggling ever since losing her."

"A replacement for his mother?"

"Yes," the woman said. "His mother died in an accident soon after he was born."

"Hold on a second. Then who're you?!"

As the sun set, the air grew cold and clear.

In exchange, the moon showed its face, the streets gradually dissolved into darkness, and the artificial lights began to shine. The color of the landscape shifted as if the sky were bleeding into the rest of the world.

Itadori walked through the night, passing the streetlights that dotted the city. The moon looked brighter than usual that night.

Curses existed in the world. They filled human life to overflowing like a darkness that could swallow even shadow. Itadori couldn't exorcize all of them the way sunlight could. He was still a long way from shining even the faint light of the moon.

But for one person, he just might be able to shine the way forward, like a streetlight.

"Kairi..."

Sure enough, Kairi Minato was there, at the same time, in the same park, his gentle swinging causing the old metal to creak.

"Itadori... Good evening."

"Yeah, hey."

For a little while, they left it at that. Itadori sat beside Kairi on the decrepit swing set. When he touched the playground equipment, which was cold in the night air, a chill sunk into his bones. As this sensation swept through him, he gazed out at the park. It presented a forlorn scene.

The only sounds were the chirping of insects in the grass and the creak of the swing. Itadori and Kairi swung gently, looking forward instead of at each other. Their rhythm was like a metronome measuring the right time for broaching a topic.

Finally, Itadori asked, "The demon's still at your house, right?"

Kairi nodded without looking at his companion.

"Probably. I think it's *always* there. At the house."

Kairi's voice was soft but exhibited an unyielding strength. His voice was low, as if reaffirming an immutable reality.

"Your grandmother told you about that demon." Itadori said gently.

"Who told you that?"

"Your *mother*."

The resulting expression on Kairi's face was difficult to describe. He looked bitter, and also as if someone had prodded a wound. It was clearly an unpleasant topic for him, but Itadori continued talking.

"Sorry if you don't like to call her mother."

"Seems like you heard they're not my real parents."

"I should've noticed sooner, since the sign out front said Okazaki, not Minato."

"I didn't mean to hide it. But I'm not used to my new name, so I said my old family name," Kairi said.

"Yeah. I can understand that."

Kairi was mumbling, like a scolded child. By contrast, Itadori's voice was buoyant and gentle.

"Your grandmother taught you that a demon shows up around bad children, right?"

"Uh-huh," Kairi responded.

"Why do *you* think that demon shows up?"

"Um..."

A few moments stretched between his words. It wasn't because Kairi was at a loss for an answer, but because the answer was so clear, he needed the courage to give it voice.

Eventually, Kairi looked down as if to hide his face and answered. "Because I'm a bad boy."

"How so?"

"I'm not related to Mr. and Mrs. Okazaki by blood. But we lived in the same neighborhood, and Grandma and I were friends with them. When Grandma died, I didn't have any relatives left, so Mr. and Mrs. Okazaki took me in. I don't think I should be there, though."

"It's not that you don't *want* to be there?" Itadori said.

"I'm not their family. They're just being considerate. They feed me and send me to school, but I'm afraid that I'm bothering them."

"I see."

For a little while, Itadori didn't say anything. He wasn't so much organizing his thoughts as taking the time to build up his determination. At last, he sighed deeply and spoke. "*You* put that curse there." Itadori looked directly at Kairi for the first time. "And since you put it there, only you can get rid of it."

"Me? No, I can't! Anyway, what do you mean that *I* put it there?!"

"What if your family is in danger?"

The sound of swinging stopped.

Kairi turned unsteady eyes on Itadori. They were full of a fear greater even than when he had looked upon the demon.

"What do you mean?"

"That demon is always stationed at your house, right? Maybe you are afraid it could attack Mr. and Mrs. Okazaki?" Itadori asked.

"No way! It threatens *me*!"

"But the one it attacked was *me*. Can you guarantee it won't hurt someone else? After all, you do like the Okazakis, right?"

"Well..."

"Your fear gave birth to that curse," Itadori explained. "If you want me to shut up, fine. But if you want to go home, you gotta work with me before there's no place left for you to go home *to*."

Itadori got off his swing and stood in front of Kairi.

As a streetlight shone behind him like a spotlight, he extended a hand toward Kairi. "I hate to admit it, but I don't think I can beat that demon alone."

Just then, the clock struck nine thirty.

Kairi took the hand that Itadori had offered and got off the swing.

They ran toward the house.

Itadori was hung up on what Kairi had said. The boy didn't think the demon would attack other people in the house? Those words echoed over and over inside his head as they ran.

Itadori coughed in the cold night air, and his heart pounded in alarm.

In the dark nighttime streets, worries assailed him. Alternating rapidly in his mind were the images of the demon that had attacked him and the faces of the family that had taken the boy in.

Rounding a corner, they entered the familiar lane. If he kept running straight, he would arrive at the house.

"Um, Itadori...?"

"Seriously? It's getting *bigger*?!" Itadori exclaimed.

They could clearly see it, even from a distance.

"Tryyyyyy agaaaaaaaaaaaaaaaaaaain."

The body of the demon, the size of a beach ball, had now bulked up to the dimensions of a station wagon. Its hulking arms spread to block the street, and the two mouths in its eyeless face were baring and grinding their teeth menacingly.

Itadori had a basic understanding of why. If Kairi had given birth to this curse, it grew larger with his fear. The boy's fear had swelled as he turned toward home, and that was making the demon stronger.

"I knew it! It's no use! I can't do it!"

Kairi turned to run away, and Itadori couldn't catch him. But he could call out toward the boy's back.

"Are you sure that's what you want to do?"

"But...but...!"

"While you're running away in fear, you could lose your home! Is *that* what you want?!"

"Ah...!"

Kairi stopped. In great trepidation, he once again stared at the street. The giant, hideous form of the demon was still there. The fright welling deep from within kept telling him to flee...flee!

However, what he witnessed in the next moment drove all thought from his head.

"Kairi!"

Beyond the demon's arm blockade stood Mrs. Okazaki.

She might have happened to step out for a stroll. Or maybe meeting Itadori had inspired a change and she had come out to welcome Kairi home. Either way, there she was, standing right beside the demon.

And the demon's attention had shifted from Itadori to her.

"Mom!"

There wasn't a moment to think. Kairi took off running, but not to flee. His feet were carrying him straight toward the house. He was running toward the person he had called "Mom."

"Tryyyyyy agaaaaaaaaaaaaaaaaaain."

The demon's gaze, which had turned on the woman, snapped back to Kairi. For the average person, the challenge of confronting a demon head-on would be like a nightmare. But Kairi didn't stop. He was more afraid of losing her than he was of the demon itself. His hastening feet thumped across the ground with increasing speed. He raced along the road, heading toward home as if to drive away the darkness filling the neighborhood.

"Tryyyyyy agaaaaaaaaaaaaaaaaaain."

"Yeah, it's about time."

A shadow passed Kairi as fast as the wind. Itadori was swinging his right fist, packed with cursed energy. The demon didn't have time to dodge. Itadori was tearing across the asphalt at top speed and at close range. He leapt under the beautiful moon.

"Divergent Fist!"

With incredible momentum, his fist bashed into the demon's face. The demon's arms, now as big around as logs, swung in an arc but were too late to stop Itadori's attack.

"Tryyyyyy—!"

Cursed energy coursed through the demon's body. Despite its size, it dispersed quickly. Just like a popped balloon, it deflated and whooshed away.

One blow from a sorcerer had removed the curse wall that had been blocking the street. The nightmarish evening had ended. Now without obstruction, the street returned to its former appearance.

Kairi was calling out. "Mom... Mom... Mom...!"

"Kairi... I'm sorry. You must have been so lonely."

Kairi kept crying, "Mom!" as if to make up for lost time.

Most likely, not every problem had been solved, but at the very least, Kairi would stop wasting time in the park.

"Thank you very much, Itadori," he said.

"No problem. Make an effort to get along with your father too, okay?"

Perhaps their farewell lasted a few minutes, perhaps half an hour. But after this exchange at the side of the road, Kairi bowed one last time to Itadori and finally disappeared inside his house. This time he wasn't alone. His mother was by his side.

Watching the two of them depart, Itadori felt a strange sensation, as if he were suffocating inside, as if he might cry. But he was just saying goodbye to someone he had saved. When they were out of sight, he looked to the side of the road, where something the size of a beach ball was rolling around.

"Why, you..."

But Itadori immediately dropped his sudden alarm.

The demon, already on the verge of death, looked at Itadori with its eyeless face. The stitches slowly came undone and its lips parted.

"Kairi is truly home now."

When Itadori spoke, the demon's shoulders shuddered. Then, with its face that was all mouths, the demon smiled broadly and vanished. Serenity enveloped the street, now that it didn't have the tumult of a fight, a mother and child caught up in the trouble, or a lurking demon.

"I think it was his grandmother," Itadori decided.

He didn't have any proof. But if it were true, Itadori thought, she must have been a cool grandma. He thought her love and worry for Kairi must have outweighed all else.

"I need to be sure I don't make Grandpa worry, either."

He had decided on his own reason to fight. He hadn't forgotten his grandfather's final words.

Now he could help many more people, and there was no time to waste.

With these thoughts, Itadori turned and started walking down the nighttime street.

"No, not just my grandfather."

Itadori was recalling his *own* death. How had Fushiguro felt when it happened? Had Kugisaki been sad? It certainly couldn't have been a *good* feeling. Itadori knew that all too well.

"I need to go home now too."

He would show everyone he was all right. With a bright laugh, he'd say there was no need to worry. This time, he would be stronger, and he would do *more*.

As his resolve firmed, Itadori's feet turned toward home. Sometimes a detour leads you back to your rightful place.

Itadori's long, long walk had finally ended.